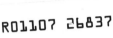

The People of the Ax

The
People of the Ax

JAY WILLIAMS

Henry Z. Walck, Inc.   *New York*

Copyright © 1974 by Jay Williams
ISBN: 0-8098-3122-8
Library of Congress Catalog Card Number: 74-5894
Printed in the United States of America

Library of Congress Cataloging in Publication Data
Williams, Jay, date–
    The people of the ax.
    SUMMARY: When he learns the significance of their
iron club, Arne is forced to grapple with the dangerous
crom, creatures that are neither human nor animal, and
their place in the world as he knows it.
    [1. Science fiction] I. Title.
PZ7.W666Pe   [Fic]   74-5894
ISBN 0-8098-3122-8

The People of the Ax

One

The buck moved slowly from shadow to sun and into dappled shade again, searching for the tender shoots that sprang from the forest floor. The light glided from the tines of his antlers and stroked his glossy hide. He was young, swift, well-fed and not as alert as he should have been. Arne sighed with pleasure.

It had been a long stalk. Arne and the old man, Melot Mother's-brother, had picked up the deer's slots in the swamp. They had followed the trail up onto the ledges, where by casting about they had at length found another hoofprint in the mossy earth at the top, and then they had seen the animal itself, moving downhill on the other side among the laurels. They had followed from a distance, keeping what breeze there was between it and themselves, and had seen it pass under the boughs of the oaks. Once in the forest, they had been able to slip closer and closer to it as it browsed until now they lay behind a thick, upflung root no more than forty paces away.

It was Arne's first deer. He had, of course, gone many times to watch a hunt or to drive deer toward a hunter. He had, from the time he had learned to draw a bow, shot birds and small game alone or with other youngsters. For a year now, since he was fifteen, he had been using the heavier bow proper to his size and strength, which were both considerable. He could drive the wicked triangular flint arrowhead clear through a plank of oak as thick as his thumb at fifty paces; it would strike deeply enough behind a deer's shoulder to find its heart. This day was his from the first cast, knowing the trails and ways of the animals, to this moment, and the kill was his. Melot had come only to observe and advise.

Slowly, Arne drew his legs under him. His head trembled slightly from the thudding of his heart. Bracing himself on one knee, he laid an arrow on the twisted brown string and nocked it. He sucked in a long breath to calm himself, but there seemed to be a fine mist before his eyes in which the deer was outlined in pale light.

It raised its head from its feeding and stood poised. *Don't move,* Arne thought, pulling the string to the corner of his mouth. He held it so at full draw, waiting. The noble antlers dropped again.

He spoke the ritual words, moving his lips but making no sound, "Forgive me. I must kill you so that we may eat." Part of his mind said, *Shoot!* In his imagination he saw the arrow speeding to the target, the leap of the deer, its blood flowing, its eyes staring at him full of liquid terror. He plucked at the string instead of loosing smoothly, let the string go and saw the arrow in reality flicker away through sun and shadow to bury itself in the grass at the deer's feet.

The beast jerked up its head at the faint *tump!* There

was, however, nothing more to startle it and it stood an-other moment and another, as undecided as Arne had been.

Arne snatched a second arrow from the quiver and clapped it on the string. His wrist was caught, as if by a striking snake, and held.

Melot Mother's-brother said, aloud, "No more."

At the sound of his voice the deer burst away and was gone.

"Let go!" Arne cried. He jerked his arm away from Melot's grasp, hurting himself. Almost in tears, he panted, "You let him get away."

"You know the rule," Melot said, mildly. "Only one shot. I am sorry about your wrist."

"Sorry?" Arne said. His voice broke on the word. "I almost had him. If I had only shot when I first drew, instead of waiting—"

He dropped the arrow back into the quiver and walked to retrieve the other. "Why?" he said. "What's the sense of the rule?"

Melot, following him, replied, "You will understand when you have a soul. Until then, you must do as you are told."

"Then I will understand soon," Arne said. His grief dropped away and he was filled with nervousness and elation. Tomorrow was the center of the year, the day of initiation. Today he was still an Unfinished Person, with a child's irresponsibility. By tomorrow night he would be fully Human, a man with a soul.

"What will it be like?" he asked, as they began to walk back together up the slope.

Melot chuckled. "You'll see. Maybe not so different from now, after all." Abruptly changing the subject, he said, "Why didn't you shoot when you first drew?"

"I don't know. I thought I was holding too high, or that he was going to move." Arne felt a little sulkiness rise in him again.

"Maybe you wanted to miss," Melot said. It was almost a question.

"Why would I want to miss?" said Arne, indignantly. "My first deer! I'm a hunter, amn't I?" He shrugged. "It's true, he was so handsome I almost didn't want to kill him. I didn't want him to move because—because I wanted to keep watching him. Maybe I'm not a hunter, Melot," he went on, suddenly anxious. "Do you think I'm not?"

Melot was nodding to himself. He said nothing, almost as if he hadn't heard Arne, but then after a moment or two grunted, "Who can tell? Maybe you'll be the best hunter of us all. When you have a soul you'll understand everything."

They reached the top of the rise, and standing on the bald, granite knob they could see, over the treetops, the restless glitter of the ocean. The air was sweet with the warm forest smell rising to them, edged with salt. Down there near the shore, hidden from them by the leaves, lay their village. A faint smudge of smoke betrayed it. They began to make their way down the ledges which fell like giant stairs to groves of oak and ash and birch.

Halfway along one tilted slab of rock, Melot halted. Earth had filled almost all the surface of the slab, and moss and little spears of ground pine grew there. Melot hitched up the handle of the ax that hung over his shoulder, and knelt. He examined one spot, pushing aside the soft green carpet. Arne craned to look over his shoulder. Two or three indentations in the moist earth, a bruised stem, nothing else. But Melot's experienced eyes recognized the signs.

"*Crom,*" he said.

Arne straightened instinctively, reaching for an arrow. But Melot touched the marks, sniffed at them, and shook his head.

"Two days old, maybe three. It stood here and looked about and went on. Maybe after deer."

The *crom* were not human, but neither were they animals. They resembled people but were hairier, often bigger and with flat eyes like pieces of slate. They were strong and furtive and above all they were full of hate. They had no souls and never would have souls and whatever else he knew about them, Arne knew, like everyone else, that they had to be killed or the world would end.

There was that kind of look on Melot's face, too. He fingered the helve of his ax and then rose.

"I don't think it is still in the neighborhood," he said. "It would have smelled the smoke of the village and gone. Let us go, too."

The village was called Strand. As they came out of the forest fringe Arne stopped to look for a moment and, as always when he came home, felt the surge of joy, the new buckling of the bond between him and this handful of houses lying in a double semicircle between woods and shore. The hills descended on the north to run out in a rocky promontory that formed the upper arm of a bay; on the south, a winding stream spread fingers through the reed beds where wildfowl nested. The houses were low and snug, of salt-stained, weathered wood and reed thatch, and their vegetable patches of maize and onions, squash and beans, were protected by low turf walls and fences of split board to break the wind. Small, graceful birches or sturdy cedars had been left to grow here and there because of their friendliness to people and their special beauty. Five hundred yards from the edge of the village the turf ended and a long sandy beach sloped to the waves. Neatly drawn up along the beach and protected by rows of wooden pilings were the canoes and the stacks of lobster pots made of woven withies. The smells of home were drying fish, discarded shells, sweet woodsmoke, seaweed and vegetable compost, a blend of dry land and ocean.

Children ran here and there swooping and screeching like gulls. Two men were splitting and stacking firewood, their axes making a slow, regular beat. Not far from them, Patok the carver was turning over pieces of wood, setting aside those which interested him. He nodded to Arne and Melot, and said, "No luck?"

"He lost it, unfortunately," Melot said.

Arne's face reddened.

"We all lose one sometime or other," Patok said, kind but abstracted, running his fingers along the grain of a likely chunk.

Melot patted Arne's shoulder. "Go and prepare yourself for the vigil," he said. "And Arne—" He looked warmly into the youth's eyes. " 'Yesterday's wave—' "

He went off. Arne knew what he meant. It was a line from the song-poem by Bakko: "Yesterday's wave, today's, tomorrow's; the same sea."

Arne walked to his own house. His father, Toke, was sitting cross-legged on a reed mat in front of the door, working on a flint with a piece of antler, whistling thoughtfully and without much tune. Flakes of stone lay about him and stone dust speckled his bare thighs. In a neat row were eight lovely barbed arrowheads, razor-edged. He was a neat, precise man.

Arne unstrung his bow. As his father raised his eyes, Arne said, quickly and roughly, "I had a chance at a perfect shot and missed it, couldn't make up my mind and shot low."

"You'll have other chances," said Toke. "Conn has been asking for you. He's at the Speech Stone. Before you go, hang up your bow, please, and don't just throw your quiver into a corner, hang it up on the peg and put the arrows—"

"Oh, I know, I know," grumbled Arne, and added, "Do you always have to tell me how to do everything?" but he said that part of it under his breath.

When he had put away his tackle, he went through the house to the summer kitchen, hardly more than a lean-to with a stone fireplace and a charcoal pit. Rows of storage pots were half buried in the cool earth along one wall. He took the lid off one and, fishing inside, picked out a strip of smoked herring and went out munching it.

The Speech Stone stood in a circular space formed by heaping up a wall of turf around a wide glade. Four entrances were cut through the wall. The stone was half a man's height, embedded upright in the ground and with a flat top. It was here that all the assemblies of the village were held, and the rule was that so long as anyone kept a hand on the top of the stone he could speak without interruption. In the distant past, the argument had been offered than an unprincipled person might force his will on others by pure long-windedness that would wear out their patience. However, the council at that time had ruled that anyone who was determined to oppose such a person would be able to wait for a turn whatever his impatience, and in any case a Human Being would find it hard, because of his soul, to behave in such a fashion. And in fact, it had happened only once in living memory, and then because an old woman had become side-tracked while discussing the location of a new midden heap and had rambled on for almost an hour, talking about her youth. Most people had simply gone politely to sleep until she had finished.

Conn, however, always made Arne feel that perhaps the council's decision had been a mistake. Tall, powerfully built, in his early twenties, with bristling, frowning eyebrows and a jaw like the Speech Stone itself, he pressed his hands firmly on the flat surface so that he seemed to be driving it deeper into the ground. He was talking steadily in a commanding voice. The ten young people who were to be initiated sat listening with glazed looks, overpowered. Lounging to one side were half a dozen of the older youths, four boys and two girls, unbothered by Conn, whispering and laughing among themselves.

". . . The question of discipline can't be stressed too much," Conn was saying. "I know you're thinking I'm making too much of it. But, believe me, in a raid everyone must follow orders and know just exactly where he's to be." His eyes flickered over Arne. "You can brag about your hunt later," he said. "Sit down, will you? We're discussing the raid on Chestnuts."

"If you could call it a discussion," Frey commented, in her clear, light voice.

Arne went and sat next to her but didn't venture to speak.

"Now, I'll go over it again to make sure everyone understands," Conn went on. "That is, if you others can be quiet for a minute, you, Dand, and Erda, nobody's really interested in your love affair. All right, then. The initiation will be finished by evening and you'll all have done the Ax Dance and you will be Human instead of a gang of Unfinished People. After the feast, about midnight, we'll set out."

"You haven't told us whether we're going to have a chance to get any sleep," put in a plump boy.

"You'll have to learn how to do without sleep, if you want to count coups." Conn ostentatiously fingered his necklace from which dangled more than a dozen pearly disks, each one marking a victorious duel. Among them hung a black cone shell which showed that, young as he was, he had already killed a *crom*. "It's fifteen miles to Chestnuts and I want to be there before first light. And I want to be there with the whole band, no stragglers. Are there any of you who have never been to Chestnuts? No? Good, you've all gone at least once with the trading carts. Then you have all seen the round, whitewashed building beyond the grain barns, which is where the Muddy Feet have their meetings. That's where the Bead Blanket hangs. There are three doors, each with a guard.

"We are going to seem to attack the storehouse. So most of us will go in that direction, letting ourselves be seen as if by accident. That will draw the guards from the west side, and once the fighting starts a team will run across the open space between the barns, as if to reinforce us but really to try to draw away the guards in the front of the building as well. At that point, two people will break in and try to get the Blanket. Now, if that general outline is clear we'll make assignments."

Arne looked out of the corners of his eyes at Frey. Her profile was serene, and she did not seem to be aware of him although the corners of her mouth tucked in mischievously. He sat up straight, thinking rather desperately that he would give anything to have her look at him with admiration.

He heard himself speaking. "Are we allowed to ask questions, Conn, or volunteer, or say anything?"

"What do you want to say?"

"I'll be one of the two who go in after the Blanket."

Heads turned toward him and he felt, rather than saw, that Frey's was one of them.

"You?" said Conn. He gave his commander's scowl, which meant that he was carefully weighing up many different questions at once and was capable of dealing with all of them. "You got your deer, did you?"

"No. What's that got to do with it?"

"You lost him? We can't afford to have anyone go in who might lose the Blanket."

Arne stood up, angrily. "The deer has nothing to do with whether I can fight, or go through a door, or—and you know it. You just like deciding things for everybody. You think you know everything."

"You see? You haven't any sense of discipline. You can't even take orders."

"You haven't given any orders," Arne almost shouted. "I'll take your orders as captain but why should you choose against me when I volunteer for something?"

His throat clenched. He spun around and began to walk away, unable to look at Frey.

Conn said, suddenly, "Wait."

Arne turned, reluctantly. Conn was gazing at him with an odd expression, so painful that Arne was taken by surprise.

"Come back and sit down," said Conn, but it was not a command.

"Well—" Arne still hesitated.

"Don't make so much of it," Conn said, irritably. "I was wrong. You can be one of the two. Who'll be the other?"

"I don't mind," said Frey.

Arne's heart gave a thump. He stared at Frey, who kept her back to him. He began to smile foolishly and sat down where he was, not even daring to return to her side, while Conn made further assignments and they planned the details of the raid.

When the meeting was over, Conn beckoned to him and to Frey. They joined him at the Stone.

"Now, as for breaking in—" Conn knelt and drew a circle in the dirt with his finger. "There is good cover among the farm buildings to the south of their meeting hall." He drew some squares. "You can work your way around toward the west side. Try to avoid duels. You want the Blanket, not glory. When you get inside the hall you'll see the Blanket hanging across the sanctuary on the north wall, where there's no door. Don't damage it when you take it down. Handle it as carefully as you would our own Horned Man. Afterwards, go right away southward, to the double line of chestnut trees outside their village, and the rest of us will meet you there. Have you any questions?"

"I think we can manage," Arne said. He glanced shyly at Frey. She stood composedly, as always, her hands behind her back, looking as though nothing would ruffle her. "I didn't mean to speak for both of us, Frey. Do you want to ask anything?"

"Suppose we're caught?" she said to Conn. "Will you try a rescue? Or shall we try to escape on our own?"

Arne looked at her admiringly. Those were the kind of tactical questions which never would have occurred to him. Obviously, if they were going to be rescued it would be wiser to wait for it and be prepared.

Conn was eyeing her with respect, too. "No," he said, "we won't be able to try a rescue. If we're to make it seem like a real raid on their storehouse, we'll have all we can do to get away ourselves."

"Good. Then we'll make our own plans."

Conn nodded. "Until midnight, then."

Arne touched his shoulder. "Thank you for changing your mind about me. I'll try—"

"You'd better do more than try," Conn said sternly and marched off, every inch a commander.

"Puffer," Frey murmured.

Arne grinned. The puffer was a fish which swelled itself up to three times normal size when it was touched.

He said, "I'm glad you said you'd go with me."

Frey smiled sweetly, tossing her heavy black braids over her shoulder with a movement of her head. "You're so helpless, you see, I thought you'd better have someone to look after you."

"Oh, really?" He began blushing again, and that annoyed him. "You needn't worry so much about me, then. I'll get somebody else."

"Poor Arne. You take everything so seriously."

"No, I don't."

"Don't worry so much. No one else will go with you. I'll see to that. You'll have me to look after you whether you like it or not."

She gave him a blazing look so full of laughter and— could it be liking?—that he could only stand open-mouthed, watching her yearningly as she walked away.

He returned home, for it was nearly noon and the vigil must begin when the sun was directly overhead. His mother, Ilot, had returned from clam digging and she and Toke ate while Arne swallowed his hunger for there would be no food for him until after the initiation ceremony. He remembered the bit of herring he had pilfered and savored it wistfully in memory. He stripped off his belt, kilt and

sandals and ran down to the sea. Most of the other Unfinished People were already there, some solemnly wash-
ing themselves, others swimming as lightheartedly as if it
were an ordinary day. These he regarded with envy for he
himself kept gulping with nervousness.

Sea-clean and tingling with salt, dressed in new green-
dyed leather kilts, their hair neatly smoothed down with
water, they all gathered at last at the Stone. They sat down
before it cross-legged and waited until Old Matte appeared
with a pot of blue dye made from the shells of a certain
snail. She was very old indeed, her hair soft and thin like
milkweed floss, her breasts mere flaps of skin. She blinked
and grinned, mumbling her lips, and with a small brush
painted at the base of each throat the ax-sign. When she
was done, they all sat in perfect silence, their minds limpid
and empty as they had long ago been taught. In this way
they could sit waiting for game for hours, aware of everything about them—the stir of mice in the grass, the flirt of
a bird's wing, the hum of flies, changes in the breeze—but
thinking of nothing. Slowly the sun moved down the sky.
Pink clouds edged with gold lay piled along the horizon.
The air thickened and twilight accumulated among the
branches outside the turf circle.

A buttery light grew in the glade. The rest of the village
was coming with torches. They thrust them into the top of
the turf bank and sat down in semicircles behind the motionless young people. As the torches burned low they
would be renewed from a pile that was already being
stacked up against a tree. The six members of the council
had taken their places behind the Speech Stone, and from

the top of the stone, by a leather thong, hung the Horned Man. This was a piece of wood cut from a section of an ancient tree so skillfully that no knot or crack marred it, although it was a full three feet wide and as many high, yet no more than an inch thick. Its surface had been perfectly smoothed and polished and it glowed with the patina of great age for it had been made long, long before. On it, in an inlay of thin, sea-worn pebbles and pieces of colored shell, was a figure half man, half stag, its human head crowned with antlers.

When everyone was settled and quiet, even the littlest, one of the council members, Barad the poet, rose. Past middle age, he was as vigorous and light on his feet as a youth and his face was unlined and full of humor. In a ringing voice, he began to recite the Tale of Shaping.

> *Out of the ending came the beginning.*
> *The dust fell together, formed mighty shapes,*
> *They of their weight swam into spheres . . .*

He chanted of the making of the earth and of the coming of life. He told how that life, by the Harmony of All Things, took many forms for the nature of life is shape-making. His voice deepened and he began to chant those lines which told of the great dance, the movement of all matter in pulses and rhythms, from the circling of the stars overhead to the changing of the seasons, the beat of the sea and the growth and diminishment of the shore, the passage of life from birth to death and so to birth again. A drum began, keeping time with his chanting, and the Unfinished People took up the words, swaying and clapping their hands in rhythm with the drum. They sprang up, one after the other, and began to dance, first each on his own, then drawing together one by one until they had formed the ring which has no end and no beginning.

Barad finished and sat down. The dancing stopped. The young people, smiling and panting, returned to their places.

Another council member, Atun the swimmer, rose. She was a splendid diver, going to the deepest places for shellfish, and her glossy black hair was cut short for that reason. In a nursery voice, she began the tale of the First Ax.

She told how Human Beings were caught in a great storm of ice and began to die of cold. Then Unkoku Father's-father and Koku Mother's-mother came to help them. With her left hand Koku cut down a tree, with his right hand Unkoku pounded it into the ground, and in this way they built a house of stakes with a roof of branches. But the ice had destroyed the crops, frozen the sea, and driven away all the animals. Unkoku and Koku began to hunt. They found a wild bull. With his right hand Unkoku struck it on the forehead and killed it, with her left hand Koku cut it up, and so they fed the people. Then Unkoku took the bull's heart, which was harder than any stone, and showed the people that at the top it was blunt like his fist, and at the bottom it was sharp like the hand of Koku. "But," they said, "if we hold it by the top we shall not be able to use that end, and if we hold it by the bottom we shall not be able to use *that* end." "Then," said Koku, "you must have another hand and hold it by the middle." She showed them how to fasten a stick to it to use as a handle. Thus the first ax was made, both tool and weapon, to build and to destroy, and to be the companion of all Human Beings.

When Atun had ended, she beckoned and eleven villagers came up to the Stone, each bearing a new ax. The iron heads shone like water under a gray sky; the wood of the helves was white and unmarred. The heads had been bartered for, twelve months earlier, from the Sea Riders in exchange for tanned deerskins, boxes of salted fish and smoked oysters, and wood carvings by Patok and his friend Atla. They were the only iron things in the village, all other tools and weapons being made from flint, antlers, bone, shell or wood.

An ax was given to each of the Unfinished People. Arne received his with awe, touching its sharp edge furtively with his thumb. The curved blade shone like a thin new moon in the torchlight.

The drum struck up again, this time accompanied by a reed pipe. The notes of the pipe, wild and shrill, stirred the blood and the young people began another dance.

In line they stamped and leaped, whirling their axes on one side and the other in figures of eight. For the past year they had used flint axes made to the same size and weight as these, learning all the art of handling them. For three months they had practiced the dance with those same flint axes, and now with the iron ones they did it with grace and ease. They flew apart in pairs and the axes made cages of gray metal around them as they struck and parried, spun in toward each other and away again. The drum beat faster, the pipe screamed, the ax-heads darted and the wooden helves met with a click. The drum gave three great thumps and they stopped. So marvelous was their skill that each ax-blade stood no more than the thickness of a fingernail from the forehead of each antagonist without a drop of blood having been drawn.

A murmur of approval passed among the villagers. Atun, who still stood in her place, gestured with both hands. Slowly the young people moved to stand before her in two files, their axes over their shoulders. Sweat ran down Arne's face and dripped off his nose. The others were as wet as he, yet none stirred.

Atun said, "Come, ax-bearers. Receive your souls."

Old Matte placed a bowl of glowing embers on the top of the Speech Stone. One by one, the young people stepped forward. As each came to the stone a lock of hair was cut from the top of each one's head with a flint knife and cast into the bowl, where it vanished with a puff and a little pungent smell. A councillor took the Unfinished Person's ax; two others, one to each arm, led the youth away into the darkness outside the turf wall and, after long moments, returned for the next. Of those that had gone there was no sign.

At last it was Arne's turn. He was, by now, trembling as much from chill because the sweat had dried on him as from fear and anticipation. The tugging of Old Matte's flint knife as she hacked off the strands of his hair made him wince away. "Stand still, ax-dancer," she said, mockingly. Barad took his ax which already, although he had had it only a few moments, he was reluctant to be parted from. Barad smiled understandingly and said, "You will have it back again."

They led him into the shadows, helping him find his way in the pitch dark until his eyes were accustomed to it. He heard whispering and the rustle of underbrush, and could make out the darker blots of tree trunks although the foliage above was so dense he could not see the stars. His feet sank into deep moss. "Lie down," said one of the councillors in his ear.

He did so. He felt a smooth hand on his forehead, and fingers touched and tapped his skull as if whoever it was were making certain of the shape of it. The fingers tightened and pressed on the top of his head with such force that pain ran down on either side of his nose and exploded in his cheekbones. It seemed to him that fine threads of heat shot from the probing fingers into some spot behind his eyes, and then the fingers were withdrawn and the pain ceased.

"This one is finished," said the voice of Ness, the youngest member of the council. So it was her fingertips he had felt on his head. But what she had done he could not tell; he felt no different.

Someone helped him rise and move some paces off, and held his arm while he sat down again on the ground, still in darkness. His woodsman's senses told him that the others were nearby, for he could smell their sweat and hear their breathing although they were silent. Four more times he heard faintly the words, "Lie down," and "This one is finished." Then Ness said, in a normal voice, "Is that the last?"

"Yes. Eleven."

She gave a long sigh of evident relief, and remarked, "I'm glad of that. I'm exhausted."

Disappointment dragged at Arne. Was that all there was to it? Except for a tiny, lingering ache on the top of his skull he was unchanged.

A hand touched his shoulder. "Stand up." He rose, and felt the others pressing around him. "Join hands," said Ness. Arne groped about him and found other hands.

They walked, linked together, out of the darkness into the open place before the Stone. The whole village was standing, waiting for them. They were made to face each other in couples. Arne found himself opposite Gito, a boy with a bony face and bat ears, with whom he had often gone hunting small game. They grinned shyly at each other as they were told to clasp hands.

Barad stood at one end of the double file, his teeth shining. He cried, in a loud, thrilling voice, "Welcome! Welcome!"

A shout went up, full of joy, a loud shout from every throat that made the torches blink: "Welcome!"

The hairs rose on Arne's neck. He stared into Gito's eyes and suddenly he knew what Gito felt.

Before this moment he had been able to know with his imagination what others felt, when his mother was displeased or when his father was proud of some good shot he had made with the bow. This was different. It was as if that shout of rejoicing had opened a bright, clear space in his mind into which Gito came for a dazzling second. It was not imagining but *knowing* with exactness Gito's pain and trepidation, and their merging into the delight everyone took in his becoming Human. And more, he knew that Gito felt as he did and shared his emotions.

In that split second he remembered Conn, earlier that day, changing his mind. He recalled the look of pain with which Conn had called him back and understood that Conn had known in just this way how he had felt.

So, too, was every Finished Person linked, through hand-clasp and shout and eye, in the same way, for now they shared the common attribute of humanity: they had souls.

Two

The raiding party lay hidden along the double row of giant chestnut trees which gave the village of farmers its name. From here they could see the cluster of thatched roofs above stone walls in the gray dawn, and catch the whiff of manure. To the right were the strips of wheat and oats, and the hayfields ready for mowing. A goat bleated; on the pale, cool air two crows climbed heavily, cawing.

Arne, propped on one elbow, lovingly fingered the handle of his ax. Absent-mindedly he worked with his tongue to dislodge a shred of broiled fish from between two teeth. They had eaten such a feast as came only twice a year, once on the day of initiation and again at New People, which was held on the shortest day of the year in celebration of the children born during the preceding twelvemonth. Sometimes, during the hungry months of winter, they had sustained themselves with the memory of the one and anticipation of the other.

There had been songs, the speaking of poetry, the giving of gifts, and many embraces and congratulations for the young Finished People. Arne had found that his new soul was not always awake; it did not, as he had at first wondered, make him aware of the emotions of others all the time. He could not force it to work, so to speak, so that he felt what others felt, but—or so his father had patiently explained to him, without stopping from neatly cutting up a slice of venison and eating it so that no drop of juice was lost—only in moments of some stress, or some excitement or passion would it come into being. "You will be surprised by it," Toke had said.

"And the deer I missed? If I could feel that way without a soul—perhaps I'll never be able to hunt?" For he had realized by then that Melot had been right; he had missed because he had wanted to out of sympathy for the animal.

"I have a soul and I hunt," Toke had answered. "We cannot feel the emotions of beasts. But we are aware of them as living things, and we only take their lives to feed our own, as some of them do as well—the great cats, or the hunting birds. That is why we are allowed only one shot, no more. In that way, the Balance is kept."

"Next time you'll hit it," Melot had put in, affectionately, heaping another ladleful of mussels on Arne's wooden platter. "The way you felt showed only that your soul was strong, and more than ready to be awakened."

It had been difficult after such feasting for the eleven initiates to leave comfort and join with Conn and the eleven older youths of the raiding band, but at last they had set out. At the beginning, some of them had stumbled and complained, yawning over full bellies, and Conn had had to bring them up sharply with the warning that he would send them home. The older ones had joked and lent helping hands, and eventually they had settled down to traveling in earnest. The darkness of the wood offered no great obstacle to them, born as they were in its shade, and they were in position before the sky began to lighten.

Frey, beside Arne, was on her knees studying the village. She whispered, "When were you here last?"

"I don't remember. A couple of years ago, with the trading cart, to get flour."

"I was here two months ago. So perhaps I'd better lead."

"All right."

Conn came crawling up to them. "You two will go last," he said, softly. "I'm taking the first party up now. You know which way to go?"

Frey nodded.

Conn stood up and waved. He set off at a trot, ax in hand, through dew-soaked high weeds toward the village. Most of the band strung out after him. They bore toward the left. A moment later the second group, five in all, led by Dand, followed. Arne took up his ax. He was prickling with excitement. Frey looked at him with a smile, and the spark of understanding flashed between them. Then they ran across the open space after the others.

Frey bore to the right. They leaped a wooden fence and stopped beside a long stone building. Edging along it, they peered around its corner.

It was a stable, holding eight of the strong, short, hammer-headed ponies used for plowing and carting. The smell of hay and horse was strong, and Arne with difficulty kept himself from sneezing. Across the way were two other buildings, their doors, like those of the stable, folded back on leather hinges. One held wagons and plows with iron shares, the only iron apart from their axes that the villagers used. The other was a workshop and toolshed, hung with flint-edged scythes and wooden rakes, shovels and forks. Frey pointed. Arne nodded, and they darted across to the narrow lane between the buildings. Squeezing along it, they came to another low railed fence beyond which were three wooden buildings set on mushroom-shaped stone legs, defenses against rats.

"Grain barns," Frey whispered, in Arne's ear.

They stepped over the fence and slipped along the side of one of the barns. On their right, across a wide open place, stood a windowless circular building, very large, its stone walls whitewashed, its conical roof of golden thatch rising above the other roofs. It stood a little apart from the rest of the village. To the left, as they faced it, were other grain barns in a row and then houses, built snugly side by side. Arne, remembering when he had first seen this village, was struck again by its strangeness, all huddled together behind barns instead of open to the reaches of shore and sea.

Craning forward to look over Frey's head, he could see the door at the side of the meeting house. There were two guards, both girls, sitting with their backs against the wall, dozing. Instead of leather kilts, they wore one-piece cloth garments with short legs and no sleeves. Even as Arne watched, a sudden clamor broke out off to the left among the houses, and the guards snapped awake and came to their feet, axes ready, in a twinkling. One of them said something and ran off; the other hesitated, doubtfully.

They could see her turn toward the door and away again, and then she made up her mind and ran after her companion.

They could hear the rattling of ax-handles and some shouting. Into the open space ran the five others from Strand, the support party. They jostled together, making sure they would be seen, and then sped toward the houses. From the right, from the front door of the meeting house which Arne could not see, came two more guards, a boy and a girl, in pursuit.

"Just as we planned," Arne could not help exclaiming.

Frey was already bounding across to the unguarded side door. He ran after her. He pushed against the door; quicker than he, she had seen the wooden knob, slid it to one side, and they tumbled in.

The circular room was full of shadows, but they now saw that spaces had been left between the top of the stone wall and the beams of the roof, through which light filtered. That light was faintly golden and Arne realized with half his attention that the sun must just be rising. Woven hangings patterned in muted orange, ocher, deep blue and crimson softened the wall. The floor was hard, beaten earth, covered with thick straw mats. Opposite the door they had come in by was the eastern door, presumably still guarded, on the right, the southern door; on the left, hanging before an alcove in the wall, the Bead Blanket they had come to steal.

It was made of thousands of tiny beads cut from colored shells, sewn on a linen backing some three feet square and depicting a thundercloud, streams of water, and a woman holding ears of ripe grain in one hand and a cup in the other. The light played across its surface which shone as if wet. It hung by loops from a wooden pole set across two pegs.

Stretching up, Arne could just touch the pole. He lifted one end of it free and as he brought it down the Blanket slid, clashing faintly, into his hands. It was heavier than he had expected and he almost dropped it.

"Careful!" squeaked Frey, involuntarily.

Remembering what Conn had said, they spread it out carefully on the floor and as carefully rolled it up. They were just straightening when a bright shaft of light burst into the chamber, and the eastern door flew open with a bang.

The guard who entered stood in the doorway, the sun throwing his shadow halfway across the floor, the dazzle of light making him look enormous. He was motionless for a second or two, letting his eyes grow accustomed to the dimness, and then he spotted them.

"You'd better surrender," he said. "I've sent my partner for help. You haven't a chance."

Arne pushed the rolled blanket into Frey's arms. "You're quicker than I am," he said. "And smarter. I'll hold this fellow as long as I can. Get the Blanket away."

The guard at once started toward them, swinging his ax. Arne ran at him from the side so that he had to turn or be outflanked. As Arne came, the guard did something which almost finished the fight. Sidestepping, he let his ax fly out suddenly toward Arne, the handle sliding through his fingers until it was stopped at the very butt end. Arne, taken by surprise, just managed to throw up his own weapon and more by luck than skill deflected the blow. He all but lost his footing and so did the guard; they tottered together, recovered and sprang apart, both with their axes held across their bodies in the first position of defense. Looking over his opponent's shoulder, Arne saw that the western door stood open and that Frey was gone.

He fixed his eyes on those of the guard. Both of them were grinning with the exhilaration of combat. The guard was perhaps two or three years older, with a longer reach than Arne's, but not quite so powerful. They circled each other, feinting. Arne made a cut, the guard parried and returned it; their ax-handles clacked together and rebounded.

And each knew what the other felt, had known it from the very first instant of engagement. Each one's mind was filled not only with his own tension and determination, but with the other's as well.

Once more, there was a rapid exchange of blows, each blocked with ax-head or upper helve. The guard feinted at Arne's shoulder, reversed his stroke and swung from the other side. Arne ducked, the blade hissing over his head. The missed stroke made the guard stagger and Arne, rising, chopped at his opponent's head in riposte.

As he did so, in a blinding instant, he felt himself stand where the other stood. With vivid reality he saw the ax fall, felt the blow cleave his forehead, the smash of pain. And now all the skill gained in months of practice, in dueling and in learning the Ax Dance, came into play, all designed for just such a moment as this, for no Human Being with a soul could take the life of another. Miraculously he checked the force of his blow as it descended. The upper point of the crescent ax-blade just barely touched the cheek of the guard, and a tiny drop of blood started out.

The guard stepped back, lowering his ax.

"Yours," he panted, ruefully.

"Thanks. A good—fight," Arne replied, equally breathless.

It was even better than a hunt, this adventure. It was like a last-minute reprieve, it filled you with an even deeper appreciation of how precious life was. As you grew older you took no part in raids, but when you were young you needed danger, it helped you to understand your place in the Balance of all things.

The guard opened the pouch which hung from his belt, and took out a disk made of pearly oyster shell. On it was painted the Grain Woman, the sign of his village. He handed it to Arne, who put it in his own pouch. Later it would go on a thong around his neck, the first of his coups.

As they smiled at each other, they became aware of shouting outside. The guard said, "They've caught your friend. It was a brave—"

Arne stopped him with a raised hand. "That's not it," he said. "Listen!"

They could hear the shouting more clearly now. *"Crom!"* somebody yelled. *"Crom!"*

They stared at each other and made for the door. Outside, the raiders from Strand and the villagers were running shoulder to shoulder toward the fields. From somewhere in the village came the deep baying note of a horn.

Conn loped by with long strides, chin high, teeth bared. Arne sprang after him.

As they reached the earth bank that ran alongside the wheat, they fanned out, some on the bank itself, some waist high in the wheat field, stumbling over the furrows, some running out to one side where they could make greater speed on the turf. At the far edge of the field Arne could see a cluster of dark figures trampling the grain or laying it flat in great swathes with bludgeons. As the foremost villagers reached them, they spread apart and ran to meet them. There must have been more than a score of the *crom,* a rarity, since they usually roved singly or in small bands or families—an old male, four or five younger ones, and a few females and cubs. Several such bands must have joined together for this attack. They outnumbered the first group of villagers, some of whom went down under the clubs.

In another moment, however, the rest of the farmers, their ranks swelled by the Strand party, caught up. The *crom,* all adult males, still fighting, began retreating to the forest which pushed out its borders to the fields on the north.

Arne, running diagonally across a corner of the wheat field, came suddenly face to face with one of the creatures. He had only seen them dead, or from a distance when they seemed hulking and slow. This one whirled as Arne caught up with him and without pause launched so swift a blow at him with a knobbed club that Arne, unable to parry with his ax, just barely escaped by springing back. The *crom* snarled at him and its smell, acrid and hateful, sickened him. It was a head taller than he was but stood hunched, its long arms dangling below its knees. Its head and body were covered with coarse, rusty hair and its face, what could be seen of it, might almost have been human but for its savage expression.

Arne knew that he should attack at once and kill the thing without delay. He knew how it should be done—a feint, a flashing double-looped swing, a bitter chop. The *crom*'s wooden stick was no match for the iron of an ax. And yet, Arne did not move except to dodge a second blow from the club.

The trouble was that the creature's eyes were so nearly human. And there was fear in them along with the hatred. It knew that none of its strength could help it against the ax, which could cut its weapon in two. That fear made it brother to the deer Arne had been unable to shoot.

But like the deer, it had no soul. He could imagine its emotions but he could not feel them, and there came from its mind no flicker of response to his.

As he hesitated, it whipped back its club and struck at his head with all its might. Automatically Arne parried, guarding his face, the keen edge of his ax ready to meet the club. There was a clang, shocking because so unexpected. The ax was dashed from Arne's grip.

In the same instant, Conn rushed up from behind. Before the *crom* could stir, Conn's weapon caught it in the chest and it fell backward. It tried to rise, staring at Arne, gave a breathless gasp, and sank down shuddering as the life went out of it.

"Lucky for you I was in time," said Conn.

Arne could not answer. That last look the *crom* had given him had been like a cry for help.

Conn eyed him, half sympathetically, half mockingly. "The first *real* fight is always a jolt," he said. "Cheer up. This one—" he pushed the body with his foot "—was the last. We got all but two or three who managed to reach the woods. I watched you and only interfered when I saw him disarm you. You must be quicker to strike next time."

He walked over and picked up Arne's ax. He puckered his heavy brows and gave a low whistle. Arne took the ax from him and stared at it in horrified astonishment.

A part of the sharp edge was folded back on itself like paper, and there was a curved nick in it deep enough to put your finger in.

Conn muttered, "I don't see how . . ."

He fetched the *crom*'s club. "Look here," he said. "That's what did it."

The club, Arne saw, was not wood but iron. That was why it had clanged when it struck his ax.

"I don't like this," Conn said. "Where would the *crom* get iron? We'll take this back to show the council."

"What about my ax, Conn?" Arne asked anxiously, as the other started away. "Can it be mended?"

"Not by me," said Conn. "Come along. You can ask the council when we get home. Oh—did you get the Bead Blanket?"

Arne told him what had happened.

"Well done. I haven't seen Frey. We were being hard pressed when the alarm came."

They joined the other Human Beings. Some, wounded,

were hobbling or being carried back to the village. Others were inspecting the damage to the wheat, or cleaning their axes, or gathering together the bodies of the *crom* to be burned.

"Look at that," said one of the farmers, shaking his head over the trampled grain. "They came only to destroy, not to steal. That's their way. Senseless!"

"A good thing for you the *crom* showed up, isn't it?" another said to Conn. "We'd have taken you all before you ever got into the storehouse."

"Go look for your Blanket," grinned Conn.

"Why—"

"So that was it," said a broad-shouldered young villager. "The attack was only a feint. You devil, Conn! What have you done with it?"

"It's quite safe," Conn said airily, although he himself didn't know where it was.

He rounded up the members of his band. All had taken part in the fight against the *crom,* and two of the older ones, Dand and Erda, had killed one between them. Many had lost their disks to the Muddy Feet in the sham attack on the storehouse and showed the small wounds of defeat on face, arm or shoulder, but Gito shyly held up for Arne the coup he had won from one of the farmers.

They walked back to the village together. The farm councillors were waiting and gravely thanked the Stranders for their assistance against the *crom.* Everyone praised them for the daring of their raid, and one said to Conn, "You can expect a raid from us before long, to get it back." However, of Frey there was still no sign and Arne, downcast over his ax, wondered gloomily what had happened to her. The councillors examined the iron club and agreed with Conn that it should be shown, with Arne's ax, to his own council.

"It is your trophy, after all," said one. "I don't think we shall see the *crom* return for a while, but perhaps we'll go looking for them. If they have found a way of getting iron we may have trouble in store."

The Strand people said farewell and began the homeward march. When they came to the double line of chestnut trees at the edge of the village, they halted. Frey was seated at her ease, her back against one of the trunks, the rolled blanket in her lap.

"You look surprised to see me," she said to Conn. "But this is where you told us to meet you when we had the Blanket."

"Good work," said Conn, unable to keep his expression of stern leadership from sliding into a smile. "You missed a brush with the *crom.*"

"I heard the alarm," she said, getting up. "But I wasn't going to leave this trophy behind and I knew there were enough people to deal with them without me. Here, you can carry it, it's nice and heavy."

Conn asked one of the older youths to take the Blanket. Frey, going to Arne, said, "You look as if you'd lost the duel."

He shook his head. "I won."

He held out his ax. She examined it, wincing in sympathy. "How did it happen?" she asked.

"One of the *crom* had an iron club."

"Oh, Arne. I am sorry. Can it be repaired?"

"I don't know."

The party was moving on, and Conn said, impatiently, "Come along, you two." Frey took Arne's hand.

They stood looking at each other while the rest left them behind. Everything that needed to be said was said through their eyes.

At last Arne, squeezing her hand, said, "You won't make fun of me?"

"Not about this. But may I still laugh at you now and then?"

"You can do anything you like," he replied ardently.

"We'd better go after the others."

He held her back. "It's true, isn't it? About us?"

"Yes."

He laughed happily. "Then I don't mind about anything else, not even the ax."

Still holding hands, they hurried to join their comrades.

By road the way was much longer, but in daylight as quick as going through the forest. They reached the village before noon and after being welcomed and admired for securing their trophy, most went off to their homes to eat and sleep. Conn and Arne, however, were taken apart by the council for a talk. They sat down on the short grass that grew from a dune above the beach. It was a clear, hot day with little wind, and the waves broke with a soothing hush. Conn showed the iron club and Arne's ax, and the councillors put their heads together over them.

Getsu, who was Old Matte's husband, older even than

she was, but with a memory still clear and sharp, said, "Did others of the *crom* have such clubs?"

"This was the only one I saw," said Conn. "But a couple of the *crom* got away. I don't know what they had."

Calth, an expert tracker, said, "And you, Arne, didn't you see that the club was iron when you fought the *crom?*"

"No. I mean, I didn't think of it. It was shaped like a club and I only thought of it as a club."

"If the *crom* have found a way of getting iron—" said Atun the swimmer, and let the unfinished sentence hang ominously above them.

"Perhaps not, perhaps not," said Barad. "Let's not make a school of cod out of one dead fish."

Getsu tapped the club. "This is no mere lump of metal, you see. It has been molded or worked to have a handle and a knob. Can we believe that the *crom* made it? Eh? Would anyone in the world make one for them—and at what price?"

He peered around at the others, blinking his little, bleared eyes. No one answered.

He turned to Arne. "Tell us about this *crom* you fought, my boy, everything you can remember. Everything that happened, from the beginning."

Arne did so, as best he could. When he had done Getsu flapped a hand.

"Go away, Conn," he said. "We don't need you. See that their Bead Blanket is treated with reverence and stored away. Arne, go and sit on the beach and listen to the sea for a little while."

Obediently Arne walked away and began throwing

pebbles into the waves. Over his shoulder he could see the councillors talking earnestly together. After a few moments Atun beckoned to him.

When he was seated before the council again, Getsu said, "We cannot repair your ax. We have no metalsmith here capable of such work, nor has any village we know hereabouts. The ship of the Sea Riders will be here in a few days. We can send the ax with them to Red Stones, the village where it was made. They are all smiths there."

Arne, with a sinking heart, said, "How far away is it?"

"A long way. Seven days' sailing down the coast to a place called Havens. That is where the people of Red Stones send their goods for trading. Then inland to the mountains where they live, many miles, I don't know how many days. The Sea Riders will take your ax to Havens where it will have to wait until some of the people come there from Red Stones—"

"It could take months!" said Arne. "And all that time I'd be without it." And desperately he added, "I'll go with it. I'll take it there myself."

Getsu nodded, as if he were not surprised by this. "You could do that. The Sea Riders would take you to Havens, and you could make your way to Red Stones. It will not be easy."

"I don't care. I'd rather do that than sit about here, waiting."

"Yes, so we thought. In that case, we would ask you to visit someone on the way and tell her about this." Getsu laid his hand on the iron club.

"Someone? Who?"

"Her name is Osan. She lives alone, high on the shoulders of a peak called The Pale Woman which rises among the mountains where Red Stones lies. I do not know where it is, but someone along the way will be able to tell you how to find the peak."

"Very well," said Arne. "Shall I take the club with me?"

"You'll have a difficult enough time without dragging that along with you," smiled Barad. "All you need do is describe it to Osan and tell her all that happened, as you told it to us."

"Yes," said Getsu, "and when you see her, give her this from me."

He took from his belt pouch a flat disk made of some yellow stuff which was very heavy and as silky as a sea-polished pebble. On one surface was engraved an eye, on the other an ax.

"You may find her hard to talk to," said Getsu. "She is a strange woman. This will make her listen."

Arne put the disk into his pouch and picked up the damaged ax.

"I'll go home now," he said. "I'm very tired."

"Yes, go and rest. You did well on the raid, you and Frey," said Atun. "We'll talk to you again tomorrow and give you what help and information we can for your journey."

Arne bowed his head respectfully and left them sitting there. He walked slowly and painfully through the soft whips of grass, his legs trembling with fatigue. Now that everything was settled, he tumbled from the events of the last twenty-four hours and more into pure weariness. He could think of nothing but dropping into bed.

A figure rose from behind a candleberry bush. It was Frey. She put her cool hands on his shoulders, and he gripped her wrists to keep himself from falling down asleep.

"I watched you talking to them," she said. "Open your eyes, Arne! What has happened? What was decided?"

"I am going away," he said. "I have to take my ax to be mended. Far away, to the mountains, and first by sea. I must leave you, and I've just found you."

She shook him. "Look at me," she said.

He blinked at her. It needed no soul to feel her concern and love.

"Do you think I'd let you go alone, you idiot?" she said. "I'm going with you."

Three

The ship came heaving in on the morning tide like a broad-beamed but graceful swan. The resemblance was increased by the carved bird's head that arched above her bows, and the shielded paddle wheels on either side. Gulls wheeled over her, screaming. Being of shallow draft, she stood in close and dropped anchor. Her boats were lowered and were escorted in by children who ran splashing into the water and swam around them like so many porpoises. The whole village was on the beach waiting to greet the seafaring traders.

Everything about them was deliciously curious: their weather-beaten complexions, the carved wooden plugs they wore in holes in their earlobes, their uncertain walk as if the ground were moving under them, the short tarred trousers both men and women wore against the wet, and the tang of their speech seasoned with unfamiliar phrases. They wore no axes, only hatchets or sheath knives of iron on their belts; there were no *crom* in the waste of waves.

Their captain was a trimly-built little woman with a broad face and round eyes that gave her a catlike look. She came up the beach to where the councillors stood and said, with a laugh, "Well, well, you sand-skirkers, still here, eh? You haven't been washed away by the tides yet?"

"Welcome, Setuka," said Barad. "It's good to see you again. I hope your voyage has been pleasant and successful."

"Pleasant enough, with the clear weather and favorable winds. But—successful? How can it be, with all you villagers as greedy and grasping as you are? You're too hard bargainers for us poor drifters."

She shook her head sadly and the councillors chuckled, for everyone knew the saying, "As shrewd as a sailor."

"Yes, yes," said Barad. "We'll do our best not to fleece you, we won't even charge you for your dinners. Shall we eat first and then unload?"

"By all means," said Setuka. "We've had light airs the last day and a long tread, and we're as empty as the Sea Lord's barrels." And she laughed merrily again, so that Arne, watching, thought she must be a simple and light-hearted person.

He changed his mind when he watched her bargaining. Her face then closed up like a mussel at low tide, and she haggled without a hint of a smile over every detail. Each ship of the Sea Riders was a common enterprise with everyone sharing in the profits, and the chaffering was between Setuka and three others of the crew on one side, and the village council on the other, with anyone else from the village or the ship putting in a word whenever they felt like it, so that at times the beach sounded as if a flock of starlings were squabbling there. It was, after all, not only business but entertainment. The seafarers had cloth to trade, bright-dyed wool and rough linen, wine, olive oil in clay pots—the pots themselves valuable after the oil was gone, cakes of dried fruit, and albums of lovely paintings of mountains, waterfalls, and old trees done in melting ink, the work, they said, of a man named Juda who was also a potter. To add to the noise and confusion, carts arrived later in the day from Chestnuts and two other inland villages, with beechwood bowls and spoons, scarves woven of soft goats' hair, honeycombs, and the famous barley bread of the village of Willows which stayed fresh for weeks and was much sought after by travelers.

When all the dickering was finished, Getsu drew the captain aside, with Arne and Frey. "Can you take two passengers to Havens?" he said. "And without making too hard a price, to oblige me? These two have a grave errand to accomplish."

Setuka looked them up and down, and nodded. "Just to oblige you, Getsu. They can come in exchange for their legs."

Arne stared at that. "Don't look so scuppered, boy," she chuckled. "We're not going to chop them off. It's the paddle wheels I'm talking about. We can always use another couple of pairs of legs."

The Sea Riders rested on shore that night. In the morning they loaded their ship and filled their water casks. Arne said farewell to his parents. All that he was taking with him was in his belt pouch and a light leather knapsack over his shoulders: a clean kilt, a second pair of sandals, a warm shirt, a leather water bottle, a wooden spoon and bowl, some spare bowstrings, half a dozen spare arrowheads. A new flint knife, his father's gift, hung from his belt in a scabbard made by his mother. His ax hung in its sling at his side, his bow was in his hand. He looked once around the tiny room, which had been his own all his life so far, and drew a deep breath to suppress the tremor that shook him. In the main room his mother kissed him, pulling his face down to hers. She pressed her forehead against his and shared with him her grief and the fear that she might never see him again. His father kissed him, and in his mind was wonder and a sense of expectation so that Arne's wretchedness fell away and he began to anticipate adventure.

They walked down to the shore where Frey joined them. Her mother was still fussing over her, smoothing her hair and tightening the thongs of her knapsack, but her father was silent, his eyes red and puffy; she was his darling.

They were paddled out to the ship in one of the canoes, and Setuka leaned over the bulwarks of the ship and shouted, "Come on, come on. The tide won't wait for your good-byes."

The two scrambled up the rope ladder which was pulled in after them. The ship was by no means unfamiliar to them for when younger, like all the children of the village, they had explored it or others like it each time the Sea Riders came to trade. They were sent below and shown the corner where they were to sleep. There they dropped their gear and were sent to take their places, side by side, on the treadmill that drove the starboard paddle wheel. On deck Setuka was beside the tiller. At her command the anchor was hauled in. A second command, and the wheel master on the deck below her shouted an order through the opening in the deck. The gangs hauled on the levers which engaged the cogs—these and the anchor were the ship's iron. The cogs increased the drive of the paddle wheels. Then the walkers, three abreast and nine to each wheel, began their goalless climb within the cages of the treadmills. The wheels creaked and began to turn with a churning noise. The starboard walkers were facing aft, the larboard ones forward, and as they walked the ship turned on its own length. Then the starboard walkers faced about and both wheels began thundering again as they moved southward along the coast.

The crew on watch walked for two hours at a stretch, when necessary, but today a fresh breeze sprang up after less than an hour and Setuka had the cogs disengaged. The big, square mainsail came rattling down, was sheeted home, and bellied out to the wind. Then Arne and Frey could go off to rest. Their leg muscles, unused to such work, were sore and stiff.

Arne massaged his calves and said, "Are you homesick?"

"I'm too tired to be homesick," Frey replied. "I wonder how often we have to walk in that wheel?"

"Maybe only when they find us. We could stay out of sight."

Frey looked about. They were in a long low space forward of the starboard wheel, lighted by an open hatchway down which spilled the sun. "I don't think I want to lurk down here. It's not very interesting. Shall we go on deck?"

"As soon as my legs stop whimpering and will hold me."

A shadow crossed the open hatch, and someone came quickly but heavily down the steep companionway. A thickset man, his body corded with muscle like the bark on some old tree, approached them. He had a short, dark beard, a rarity among Human Beings, which gave him a *crom*like look. However, his face was friendly.

"I'm Askar, the Chief. Everything all right?"

"Yes," said Arne. "But I thought Setuka was the captain."

"So she is. She has the *ardetlat,* after all. My job is looking after the crew. I wanted to make sure you were settled. You lash your hammocks to these beams."

He produced from under his arm two tightly-rolled hammocks made of woven fiber and showed them how to hang them from wooden pegs on the beams above and how to stow them in racks when not in use.

"You'll mess and sleep with the second watch," he explained. "As for work, you'll walk with them as you've already done, when we're using the wheels, but you're excused all other work. After all, you know nothing about it, do you?"

"No," said Arne.

The Chief's voice was kindly but also a little condescending. "It wouldn't do for you to grab the wrong rope. So when you're not walking, stay out from underfoot. Right? Now, if you'll come up on deck, I'll introduce you to Penkoro, the master of your watch. He'll explain the details."

Arne said, "Thank you. May I just ask a question? You said that Setuka had the—something—"

"The *ardetlat*."

"Yes. What does it mean?"

"Why, it's the homing sense. Her soul has this special quality, that it can always tell in which direction we're sailing, and where our home lies. That is what makes a captain, among us. Of course, she is also a prime sailor and above all a good bargainer, and that counts for a lot, but without the *ardetlat* a ship would be lost. Now, come along."

They very quickly learned their routine and after another day had settled into life in this new home where nothing was ever still or silent. Always, the vessel creaked and groaned—that, said Watchmaster Penkoro, was a good sign for it meant her timbers were yielding to the waves so that she would ride smoothly through any weather. And always she swooped and dipped, plunging her bows into the sea which creamed and bubbled about her forefoot and dashed up glittering spray. However, both Arne and Frey were used to the bobbing of canoes and neither was disturbed by the motion. The food was plentiful and good, if rather monotonous, and since the wind held fairly steady from the north or northwest the wheels were not often used, so they were not overworked and had plenty of time—almost too much time—to lean over the rail and look at the view. The ship had made all her trading stops on the northward journey and now she bore straight for home, so Setuka had taken her wide of the coast on the most direct route. It meant they would be only seven days at sea but it meant also that there was nothing but water to look at.

The only thing that irked them was the manner of the

Sea Riders toward them. It ranged from the slightly patron-
izing, like that of Chief Askar, to the contemptuous, like
that of Perika, one of the crew members in their watch who
never spoke to them without calling them "clam-diggers,"
or "sand-grubbers," and who made it plain she didn't
think much of anyone who hadn't been born, as she put it,
with a belaying pin in one hand. As for Setuka, when she
took the trouble to notice them at all, she would smile in
her round-eyed way and say, "Still aboard, eh? Not washed
away yet?" in a way that made them feel like small children
and incompetent ones, at that.

Things became even worse on the third day.

The wind had become fluky, blowing and dying away. In
the morning it had changed, and heavy, flat-topped clouds
came boiling up from the southeast, turning the horizon the
color of slate. Lightning could be seen off there, striking
into the leaden sea now flecked with white. The storm came
marching toward them and Setuka had the mainsail furled,
leaving only the staysails to keep the ship's head to the
wind. The waves rose about them and with a scream the
wind struck, driving solid sheets of rain ahead of it.

The vessel rolled and pitched as if trying to evade the
lightning which flamed balefully on one side and the other.
Now the great wheels with their size and weight stabilized
her, although they could not be turned because of the huge
seas which laid the ship on her beam ends. Two of the
strongest of the crew hung onto the tiller and kept her bows
to the wind.

Arne, huddled below decks, felt his stomach rise and
hang suspended in midair at each roll and suddenly, shame-

fully, before he could get to the companionway, he vomited on the deck. He was too sick to care and rolled into the scuppers, while Frey, who seemed unbothered, got a mop and cleaned up the mess. Twice more it happened, and when Frey tried to comfort him he told her to go away and leave him to die.

The storm had blown itself out by midday and by late afternoon the rain had stopped. Arne's sickness passed off and he felt perfectly well again. But everyone he looked at seemed to be grinning, and even Askar's sympathy seemed to Arne to mask derision. He began to sulk and would not even talk to Frey.

The sea, as if relenting, was calm and the sun drew a shimmering path along it. Arne, with his elbows over the rail, stared westward and thought wistfully of the land which lay somewhere in that direction. He was alone; Frey had gone to help the cooks in the galley rather than be idle.

"Poor sand-grubber," said a voice above him. "The sea was too much for you."

Perika had been working with two others in the rigging of the mainmast, and she had come down the starboard shrouds which led like a ladder to the channels outside the rail. She stood with one foot on a ratline, the other on a deadeye, holding on carelessly with one hand and grinning down at Arne.

He glowered at her. "Leave me alone."

"But I'm only telling you how sorry I am that you were sick. You mustn't worry about it. We can't all be sailors, you know."

"I don't want to be, if they're all like you."

"Well, they certainly aren't like *you,* squatting on the shore in the mud, afraid to get out over your depth. Look at you, hanging onto the rail with both hands! Let go, can't you? Try a little run, like this—"

Balancing herself like a gull, she leaped to the rail and ran a few steps along it toward him. He drew back, admiring her agility in spite of himself.

At that moment, the wheels, which had been still while a shift changed, began to turn. The ship gave a lurch, and Perika went over the side.

She struck the wide shield which covered the paddle wheel and bounced off it. She fell clear of the wheel, luckily, and into the water. She threw up her hands, gasping, and went down. Her terror rang like a soundless shriek in the minds of everyone in the ship.

Others had seen her fall and were shouting, "One overside!" There was a rush of feet, and lines with floats on them went flying over while, almost at the same instant, the wheels stopped. Perika came up again farther away, too far to reach any of the lines, and floundered wildly.

Without thought, Arne sprang to the rail, dropped down to the wheel shield, and almost in the same movement dove into the sea. He had learned to swim before he could walk, and he reached her side with a dozen powerful strokes. He eluded her flailing arms and as she began to sink again caught her by the hair and pulled her up. "Lie still!" he snapped, and got his arm under her shoulders so that she could catch her breath. He towed her back until she was within reach of one of the floats and could grasp the line. She was pulled up like a fish while he, more leisurely, caught hold of another rope and walked up the ship's side. He came aboard feeling much more cheerful.

He wiped the water out of his hair with the flat of a hand. One of the crew brought him a coarse towel, others were wrapping Perika in a blanket. Frey came pushing through the crowd that had gathered, and took in at a glance what had happened.

"You're all right?" she said, running to Arne.

"I enjoyed the dip," he said.

Setuka had come down from her post on the steering deck, and with a few words sent the crew back to their duties. She said to Perika, "What happened? How did you go over?"

Perika, reddening, said, "I was playing the fool, dancing around on the rail showing off in front of him." She looked at Arne. "I haven't even thanked you yet."

He gave an embarrassed shrug.

"You know what you did, eh?" Setuka said to her, grimly. "That kind of behavior is irresponsible. Report to Askar for punishment."

Perika nodded, huddling the blanket around her shoulders. "Thanks, clam-digger," she said to Arne, with a quick grin, and made off.

"Come with me, you two," Setuka said. Arne and Frey followed her up the short ladder to the steering deck. She glanced at the sky, at the quartermaster who stood with one hand on the tiller, steering, and up at the mainsail which had been set to catch the light wind and help the paddle wheels along.

Then she said, "Do you know, it's a funny thing but most sailors can't swim a stroke."

"I didn't know that," said Arne.

"You have put us all in your debt. I don't know if there's anyone aboard who could have gone in quickly enough, or can swim well enough to have rescued her. Stupid, isn't it? I hate water, myself."

She pondered for a moment, and then said, "Would you like to be relieved of all work for the rest of the voyage?"

"Oh, no," said Frey. "Oh, well, sorry, I can't speak for Arne, but as far as I'm concerned the voyage would be horribly dull without work."

"Just the way I feel," Arne said.

"How can we repay you? There must be something we can do. Can you tell me your errand? Maybe we can help you with it."

"We have to go to Red Stones to have my ax mended," said Arne. "And we have to find a peak called The Pale Woman, to give a message to someone who lives there."

Setuka's face cleared. The Sea Riders, good traders, hated to be under an obligation to anyone which could not be balanced by repayment, and the sooner the better.

"Then we *can* help you," she said. "You would never find your way to The Pale Woman by yourselves; it is a difficult journey to get up through the mountains to the pass that leads to that peak. When we land you in Havens, I will take you to someone who will give you a map. That will make the journey simpler."

"Ah. I see. Thank you," said Arne.

Something in his tone made Setuka look at him again. She said, "You do know what a map is, don't you?"

Arne glanced sidelong at Frey, who lifted her shoulders and stretched her mouth in a comical grimace.

"Well, in fact," he said, "actually . . . no, we don't."

"Good!" said Setuka, with a laugh. "Even though you may know how to swim, you don't know everything. It'll give you something to look forward to, eh?"

The last days on shipboard passed more pleasantly than the first, for the crew went out of their way to make Arne and Frey feel their gratitude. "We are all very tight-knit, aboard," Askar explained. "More than a village, you see, because we can't get away from each other, can we? So what happens to one of our shipmates is what happens to us all." Special delicacies were made by the cooks and pressed on the pair by their messmates, who all but fed them by hand; people brought them little presents, bits of scrimshaw, amber beads or wooden earplugs; everyone smiled at them, and patted them in passing, or hurried them on deck to see unexpected sights—a whale blowing in the distance, a gambol of dolphins. "In some ways I wish the voyage was over," Frey whispered to Arne, once. "I feel too pampered. It can't be good for me."

Gulls appeared, mewing greetings, and on the evening of the seventh day they saw the sunset through pink-edged and golden clouds which rose above the land. Early the next morning the coast was near enough so that spicy scents came from it, welcome after so much brine. Slowly, as they approached, the land extended two grassy arms on which grew wind-bent trees. The hands of these arms were rocky points against which the spray dashed, and inside their shelter was a large, calm bay. They could see white, yellow or pink cubes which became houses with stone roofs.

"Havens," said Perika, proudly. She had dragged Arne and Frey away from their breakfast to see.

The watch changed, the mainsail was clewed up, the wheels began thumping. Slowly the vessel moved between the rocky headlands, headed across the bay, and with the wheels stopped glided smoothly to rest alongside a wooden jetty, one of half a dozen which thrust out from shore. Other ships of all sizes and rigs were moored to them, and sailors paused at their work to wave to the newcomers. A gangway was thrown over and the work of unloading began.

Setuka, turning over the command to Askar, told Arne and Frey to follow her ashore. They said their good-byes, and Perika brought them a bag of food so that they should not have to spend time hunting during the first couple of days, at least. "I shall think a little better of clam-diggers after this—but not too much, so don't let your heads get too big," she said.

The pair were glad they had Setuka to lead them, for Havens was an enormous town. There might have been over a hundred houses clustered around the curve of the bay and another couple of dozen lying higher up the slope, with winding lanes going among them. Near the docks were large warehouses and a public set of scales, a large beam with blocks of cut stone to balance it, for the weighing of cargoes. The streets and lanes were cleanly paved with round cobblestones. Beyond the waterfront were rows of workshops and then a large open marketplace, loud with bartering and full of unfamiliar smells. Arne was astonished to see people handing over strips of beads or shell tokens in exchange for goods, and learned from Setuka that these represented the value of shares held in ventures. "Instead of carrying goods around with us, which would be ridiculously cumbersome," she said, "each member of an enterprise is credited with his or her return and given so many tokens. We call them *lukar.*"

"But what happens when someone no longer has any —er—*lukar?*" said Frey. "What if they have used it all?"

"No one goes hungry among *us,*" Setuka replied, rather stiffly, "whatever may be the case with you villagers."

"We all go hungry together in the winter," said Frey, with a giggle. The idea of anyone in the village being full when others were hungry was too funny to contemplate.

They ascended a steep street for a little way, turned into an alley, and stopped before a narrow, high house. It had two stories, with an upper balcony built out on beams so that standing there one could look over the roofs to the water. Setuka pounded on the door, and after a moment a man came out on the balcony, looked down, and called, "Why are you making such a racket, my dear? Come up."

They went in through a large comfortable room with high-backed wooden settles piled with pillows stuffed with seaweed, a long table, a dresser on which were some beautifully made pottery bowls and cups, and in one wall a large stone fireplace. They climbed a steep ladder to a sunny, rather bare room above where the man was waiting for them. He was thin and stooped, with a big nose, and coarse, grizzled hair like that of a badger. Most surprisingly, he wore, wedged into the skin around one eye, a disk of some perfectly transparent stone, highly polished and clear, which made that eye look larger than the other. He kissed Setuka, and turned to the other two.

"This is Weikar Mother's-father," Setuka said. "And these are Frey and Arne, from the village of Strand."

"Be welcome, my dears," said Weikar. Then, with a twinkle, seeing them stare at his eye, he said, "You have never seen glass, have you? Look." He took the disk from his eye and held it between thumb and forefinger over the thumbnail of his other hand. To their amazement, the nail at once appeared to be twice as big.

"If you had as much close work to do as I have, you would be glad of such a thing," said he. "It was made for me by a most ingenious friend—" he pronounced the word *ingeniose,* drawing it out humorously "—one whom, alas, I do not see very often these days. Her name is Osan."

"Osan! That's the woman we have to visit," said Arne.

"Indeed? I hope you will not find it too difficult," said Weikar, politely.

"My mother's father means that it will be a very hard road," Setuka said, bluntly. "That's why I've brought them to you, Weikar. We owe them a favor. They'll need a map."

"A pleasure, my dear," said the old man.

There was a large worktable along the wall facing the unshuttered windows and open door that gave on the balcony, so that it had plenty of light. Stands of wax candles rested on it, as well, for those days when the weather kept the shutters closed. The table was littered with sheets of paper made from mulberry bark or reed-pith, with wooden straightedges and dividers, reed pens and pots of colored ink. Below were shelves piled high with drawings which neither Arne nor Frey could make out the meaning of.

Weikar poked among the drawings and finally pulled one out and spread it on the tabletop.

"They have never seen a map," Setuka put in.

"I see. Well, it's nothing very strange. It is only a picture of the countryside, as you might see it if you were a bird."

Arne wrinkled his brows. "A plan. I understand. You know, Frey, like the plan Conn drew for us in the dirt when we raided Chestnuts."

"Look here," said Weikar. They stood on either side of him, inspecting the lines and dots drawn on the paper. "Here, at the top of the map, is where the sun rises, marked with a circle and an arrow; at the bottom, the sunset is shown with a half circle and a line. If you place the map so that it lies along the line of the sun's passage, you can tell where you are and which way you're going.

"See here, at the bottom, this blue? That is the harbor, and here the little squares show the houses as if you were looking at them from far above. Here is the road which climbs into the mountains. And here, near the top of the map, is Red Stones, where they work iron."

"It doesn't look very far," said Frey, but doubtfully.

"No, but do you see this line I have drawn at the bottom? It represents the distance a walker can travel in a day, going at a leisurely, swinging pace. A most *ingeniose* invention of mine. Lay the top joint of your thumb along it—so. Now you can measure how far it is from Havens to Red Stones: six days' walking. They have a long way to come with their carts, for the trading."

He pointed with a flat-nailed, knobbly finger. "Here is The Pale Woman, the mountain where Osan lives. These parallel lines which run here and there show how the ground rises and falls; when they are close together it is steep, and when they are further apart it grows flatter. You can see how it rises into ridges and peaks, higher and higher, as you come into the mountains. These blue lines are streams, these little circles are woodland. So you can judge your landmarks as you go, as a sailor judges the coast and takes his soundings."

"Weikar makes our sailing charts for us," Setuka explained, and although he did not understand, Arne nodded wisely.

Weikar took up a reed pen and dipped it into red ink. At a point on the map, he drew a tiny shape like a man's profile. "Just here," he said, "four days from Havens, you will see to your right a rocky cliff that looks like this. We call it The Shouting Man. Do you see this dotted line running beside it? It is a road leading to a village of potters, called Ten Bamboos. Above that village, there is a pass leading to the high ground and so eventually to The Pale Woman. They will show you how to reach the pass, at Ten Bamboos."

He folded the map and handed it to Frey, who said with admiration, "It is a wonderful thing. Thank you, Weikar. It will make our journey much easier."

"Yes, it is most *ingeniose,* isn't it?" said he, rubbing his hands together and cracking his knuckles. "I have made charts and maps of all the coasts our people explore, and little by little I am making a map of the whole known world. It will take me years yet."

"May you live to finish it," said Arne.

"I intend to do so," Weikar answered, with a comfortable chuckle.

They took their leave of him, and Setuka went with them to the edge of the town where the road, running up from the docks, led inland. It was wide enough for four people to walk abreast, rutted from cartwheels, and dusty under the summer sun. The gently rolling ground on each side was fenced into vegetable patches, kept by the people of the town. Far in the distance, on the horizon, they could see a dark, uneven line.

"Is that the mountains?" asked Arne.

"No, no, it's the beginning of the Wild Land, the forest. From there you will see the mountains. Are you sure you will not rest in Havens today and start out tomorrow?"

"Quite sure," said Arne. "If we have so far to go, we had better do what we can to shorten the journey. Goodbye, Setuka, and many thanks."

"Nonsense. We're even now, eh? When you return, you'll need passage home. Ask for me at the wharves, and if I'm not there, go to Weikar's."

She gave them a wave of her hand and turned back to the town. They watched her trim figure receding down the hill, and then set their faces to the west.

Four

Arne, propped on one elbow, looked down at Frey asleep, the dawn pearling her cheek and the curve of her shoulder. A wave of tenderness swept over him, of fear for her safety, of desire, of amusement at the way she lay cuddled together like a child with her fist to her mouth. As if nudged by that surge of emotion she opened her eyes, turned her head and smiled at him. Since they had souls, nothing of what they felt about each other needed to be said.

"Time to get up?"

"Yes," said Arne. "We should gather some food before going on. And we have to decide which way to go."

They had traveled swiftly, so swiftly that they had taken only three days to cover the distance Weikar had said would take four, and when they had made their last camp they had seen on the right the beetling cliff whose upper part was shaped like a gaping profile. They had stretched the provisions Perika had given them, spending no time in hunting but eking out what they had with wild plants and roots, grasshoppers, and a rattlesnake they killed at their second camp. At night they had slept on the ground wherever they found themselves, making a fire pit and lying with their feet to the hot embers, knowing that few animals would approach the scents of Human Being and fire. Only *crom* might attack them and there was no way to be safe from them while asleep. It was the habit of Human Beings to accept tranquilly what could not be avoided, and the threat did not spoil their rest.

Frey pulled out the map and they studied it together. They had come up through the belt of forest into hilly country, the road growing narrower and winding among outcrops of rock. The woods thinned, and a range of low mountains filled the whole horizon. This morning as the sun rose, it touched into faint color a long stony escarpment that ran to the northwest, like a wall.

"The track to Ten Bamboos must be a little way beyond here, where we are camped," said Frey. "Shall we go there first, and on to Osan? Or first to Red Stones?"

"I suppose we had better deliver our message to Osan. Getsu felt it was important, didn't he?" Arne said. There was a note of wistfulness in his voice.

Frey giggled. "You're not much good at deception," she said. "You can't wait to have your ax made whole again."

"Well . . ."

"We'll go to Red Stones first. We have come more quickly than we expected, and if we push on we should be able to get there in two more days. It will be safer for us both if we have two good axes, won't it?"

Arne sighed with relief. "Yes, of course."

"Now, look here." She touched the map. "The road swings wide to the left, curving around a ridge, and then returns. Perhaps we can save time by cutting over the ridge to meet it."

"Good. Let's see if we can find anything to eat first."

There wasn't much. They found some mushrooms and in a rotten log, which Frey split with her ax, some grubs of the sirex beetle which had a shrimpy taste. They ate a few leaves of young plantain and dock, more to fill their stomachs than for much nourishment.

"We'll keep our eyes open for game as we go," said Arne. "Let's brace our bows, just in case."

They checked over the arrows in their belt quivers, smoothing the fletching with practiced hands. They strung their bows and each held an arrow in the bow hand, ready for the string. They had slept in a grove of beeches and they made their way back to the road and followed it until it began to make its sweep to the left. Ahead lay the ridge, shelf upon shelf of granite sparkling with mica. It dropped off to the right into a gorge which lay at the foot of the cliff called The Shouting Man, and they saw a wagon road running that way. A squared post was planted beside it on which was carved a shaft of bamboo.

"Maybe we should—" Arne began, with a guilty air.

"Now, Arne, you left it to me to decide and I decided."

"Don't scold me," he said, humbly.

They climbed the ridge easily enough, following the slant of the rocks and picking their way from shelf to shelf among low bushes and thorny blackberry canes, the berries just forming, green and hard. The top of the ridge was grassy and open and much wider than they had judged from the map. It fell away in the direction they wanted to go, however, and they began to cross it. Frey, who was in the lead, suddenly slowed, hunching her shoulders involuntarily.

A rabbit with a blue-gray coat, larger than any rabbit they had ever seen, was sitting up looking at them. It was a good eighty paces away, much too far for a certain shot. Frey began to walk to one side and Arne followed her, both nocking their arrows.

They moved at a slow but steady pace, circling the animal which kept them always in view. Imperceptibly, they began narrowing the circle, still moving around the rabbit but drawing closer to it. So long as they kept circling it, it would not run, and at last they were so close that they could see its bright, round, inquisitive eye. Arne drew his bow but Frey was quicker; before he could shoot, her arrow had caught it in the head and knocked it over.

She ran to pick it up, weighing it in her hand with satisfaction for it was as big as a hare. Quickly she gutted it and said, "Shall we eat it now or save it to cook later?"

Arne did not answer. He was staring over her head. Down the slope a little way off, a man stood watching them.

He was very broad in the chest and shoulders, heavy-looking, almost hulking. His hair hung in a tangle to his shoulders, neither combed nor braided. He wore a kilt made not of deerskin but of the striped gray fur of one of the big cats. In his right hand he bore a pair of flint-tipped spears; from a strap over his shoulder hung his ax, its blade spotted with rust. He held his head strangely, as if looking obliquely rather than directly at Arne and Frey, and it may have been this which gave Arne the uncomfortable feeling that there was something very strange about him.

He lifted his spears in greeting and came toward them, and Arne shrugged away the feeling.

"That was cleverly done. I watched," said the man.

"It's a trick we know in Strand," Arne said. "But we've never seen such a big rabbit before."

"They grow that way in the mountains. The woodchucks, too, as big as bears. And the bears . . . . Where is Strand?"

"A long way from here, up the coast."

"Are you lost, then?"

"No. We're on our way to Red Stones. I am Arne, and this is Frey."

The man nodded, and again came that odd, sidelong look, flickering up and down them. "I am Sone. Listen, why not come to my place and cook your meat?"

"We must get on," said Arne.

"It's not very far," Sone said, persuasively. "You can fill your canteens, and I could let you have some food as well for your journey. You're a long way yet from Red Stones."

"I don't know," Arne said. "What do you think, Frey?"

She hesitated. Sone's mouth twisted, and he blurted awkwardly, "Please come. I live alone and I rarely see anyone. It would give me such pleasure—"

The force of his distress and his yearning was so strong in their imaginations that they could not refuse, and yet Arne still felt uneasy.

"Are you sure it isn't far?" he asked.

Sone pointed downhill. "Half a dozen bowshots. There is a stream which flows from the hills, and that's where I have my house."

He started off as if taking it for granted that they would follow, and after a moment they did so. It was, as he had said, not far but the way was very steep, dropping sharply the last hundred yards among boulders and scree into a cool, shadowy dell full of the sound of a swift stream. Arne saw that they had in fact come around into the gorge. The rocky height across the stream must be the back of The Shouting Man. Close to the gravelly bank was a rough lean-to made of logs, no more than three walls and a slanting roof. A fireplace of stone stood before it, and nearby was a pile of firewood and a chopping block. Half a deer hung from a branch, with pine boughs tied to the exposed meat to keep the birds off. The place had more the look of a hunting camp than a dwelling.

Arne said, "You live *here?*"

Sone was arranging wood in the fireplace, and without looking up he said, "Yes."

"What do you do in the winter?" asked Frey.

"I manage," he said, carelessly. "I build bigger fires on my doorstep."

With a bow drill he quickly got some tinder alight and soon had the fire going. Frey meanwhile had skinned the rabbit and was hanging it on a green, forked stick.

She said, "Why do you live here alone?"

Sone rose, dusting his hands together. "Ah," he said. "Why? Because they won't have me, that's why."

"What are you talking about? Who won't have you?"

"Nobody," said Sone. He began biting his lower lip, his eyes turning shiftily from side to side. "They've driven me out. You find that hard to believe, don't you? You think Human Beings wouldn't treat another person that way. You're wrong."

His cheeks darkened. "They hate me. And why? Because I was badly treated, that's why. Was it my fault we were captured?"

Frey's face glowed with sympathy. She went closer to him, trying to get him to look directly at her, touching his arm with her fingertips. "We don't understand you, Sone," she said. "Who was captured?"

"My mother and I," he replied, and suddenly his words came out with a rush. "We had gone mushroom hunting. She was showing me how to tell the good from the bad. I was very young, very small. We were seized by two *crom* who had boldly come near the village. They caught my mother before she could use her ax, and dragged us both off with them. They were part of a large family. My mother—" He shrugged. "It was a long time ago. They kept me with them. I went with them wherever they wandered, for a long time, I don't know how long. I became like them. I fought with the young *crom,* and ate as they ate, and was beaten by the old ones as they were beaten."

He stared at Frey, grinding his teeth. "They were caught at last by hunters and killed, every one of them. But I was recognized as Human and taken in, and given a soul."

He was silent for a time, and Arne and Frey could say nothing, feeling the churning of his mind.

Then he went on, "But I was different. Can you under-stand that? Different from everyone else. I couldn't bear the way they looked at me or spoke to me. At last I ran away. I have lived by myself ever since, alone, all alone."

"I thought you said they drove you out," said Arne.

Sone darted a glance at him. "Did I say that? What's the difference? At least *you* understand."

As he spoke, he reached out as if to take Frey's hand. Instead he caught hold of her by the wrist and spun her around, doubling her arm up behind her back. He held her tightly so, and when she tried to struggle, he pulled her wrist higher until she cried out.

Arne, raising his ax, started forward.

Sone rapped out, "Stop! Or I'll break her arm."

"You wouldn't," Arne said. Nevertheless, he stood still. "How could you? You're hurting her."

"I know," said Sone. It was hard to say whether he was snarling or smiling. "I can kill her. And you, too."

Arne gazed at him, aghast. "But—" he said. "But you have a soul! I know you have."

It was there, like a spark among dusty ashes, a hot quick awareness. But it was in such turmoil as he had never felt in his mind before.

"I see you in my head," said Sone. "Pain . . . It's all right, you know. I have killed Human Beings before this. That's why I ran away, you see. They wanted to try to cure me, but I wouldn't let them inside. It's too painful, this way, but I can't change it."

Frey, clenching her teeth against the torment of her arm, said, "Let me go. You're no better than a *crom*."

In a conversational tone, he said, "That's right. I've taken a liking to you, though. I'll finish him off, you see, and you can stay here with me. I've been alone too long. I have to hide and put out my fire when they come along the trail from the village with their pottery. I've only been here five or six months, and I won't stay much longer. I want to go where there are fewer people. You'll go with me."

Arne came a step or two nearer. The agony in his mind was almost unbearable and mixed with it, in the most terrifying way, was a hint of the pleasure Sone took in the pain of others and in his own pain.

Sone said, "I mean it. I'll break her arm and I'll kill you anyway. Give me your ax."

Arne closed his eyes and shook his head to drive all the feeling out of it. He was just too far from Sone to reach him. And in any case, could he strike him down? Kill another person?

Not kill, stun. It would have to be very fast and unexpected, so that Sone had no warning, for there was no question he would do as he said.

And into Arne's memory came the image of his duel in the meeting house in Chestnuts, and how he had almost been couped by the guard at the very outset.

"Hand it over," Sone said, harshly. Still holding Frey's arm behind her back, he reached out with his other hand. To do so, he had to move a little sideways, so that his head was fully exposed.

Arne was holding his ax loosely with his right hand high on the handle, just under the head. He took one more step and reached it out as if to give it to Sone. Instead, he seized the butt with his left hand and shot the ax forward. It was the last thing Sone looked for, and coming straight at him like that it could not be stopped. The flat top of the ax-head took him between the eyes with a thud that made Arne shudder, for he felt the blow in his own forehead. Sone fell right down, as if all his strings had been cut, dragging Frey down with him.

She freed herself and sprang up, shivering and rubbing her shoulder.

"Oh, Arne, Arne," she said, and began sobbing helplessly.

He was in anguish, for at the last moment he had almost stopped the blow automatically, as if to give the little tap that would count him a coup, and he had had to overcome his own muscles and force himself to strike hard enough. Even now, he did not know whether Sone was dead or unconscious. He went blindly to Frey and they clung to each other for a moment or two, speechless.

Frey recovered first. She pulled away and bent over Sone.

"Is he alive?" Arne asked.

"Yes."

He relaxed.

"What are we going to do with him?" asked Frey. "We can't leave him here. Oh, Arne, what went on inside him— I couldn't bear it. I hated him but pitied him still more. I pity him now."

"Yes, but when he comes to his senses he'll try to kill us again."

Even as he spoke, Arne was pulling open his pouch. He took out one of his bowstrings and, turning Sone over as gently as he could, pulled his hands behind his back and lashed his wrists together.

Frey was looking at the map. "We must change our plans," she said. "Red Stones is too far. We'll have to take him to Ten Bamboos. We can get there before nightfall. Maybe they can help him. Certainly, they can do more for him than we can."

"But he's strong, Frey. He could run away. He might even get free. How can we make him walk?"

"I can manage that," she replied.

She untied the drawstrings of her knapsack, and took out several leather bags. She sorted through them, studying their wooden labels.

"Medicines," she explained, as Arne stooped over her. "I thought we might need some. There's wound-weal, for a festered cut, powdered greenstick for stomach cramps—I thought we might be eating strange food—and a few other things. This," she held up one of the little bags, "is temperwort. Do you know what it's for?"

"I've heard the name."

"In cases of great pain—a bad wound in hunting, say— this is used."

"Won't it simply put him to sleep?"

"You'll see. Get some water."

He filled his bowl at the stream. When he brought it to her, she measured half a spoonful of dark-brown dried leaves into it and stirred it.

"Now," she said, "we wait for him to wake up. Oh, great

Harmony!" She clapped a hand to her mouth. "We've forgotten the rabbit."

It was burned black on one side and raw on the other.

They made what meal they could of it, eating quickly, and before they were done Sone groaned and stirred. Arne went at once and supported him in a sitting position, while Frey put the bowl to his lips and said gently, "Drink." He did so, dribbling and groaning, and when he had got most of it down sank back against Arne's shoulder. His eyes were open, but glazed.

"Get up, Sone," said Frey.

He could not manage with his hands tied behind his back, but Arne lifted him. He stood swaying, quite docile, his chin on his chest.

"You'll walk with us," Frey said. "Do you feel able?"

He nodded.

"It should last until sunset," she said, to Arne. "Let's move as quickly as we can."

They shouldered their packs and took up their weapons. Arne carried Sone's ax, for they would not leave it behind for any *crom* to find. They walked upstream a little way and found a spot that was shallow enough to wade. Splashing across, they climbed and walked until they found the track leading to Ten Bamboos. Frey went in the lead and Arne strode beside Sone, holding his arm and helping him where the way was rutted. He walked like one half asleep but paced steadily, so that impatient though they were, they made good time.

The gorge opened out and a wall of rock appeared, hung like a ragged drape along the skyline. The trail kept close to the stream, which widened and ran more slowly through what became a broad valley with the mountain wall rising on one side and shaggy hills on the other. Grass with a pale blue sheen grew here, speckled with tall, nodding wild flowers, and here and there beside the water were clumps of rustling, feathery bamboo such as grew near the estuary at home, in Strand. There were junipers, too, and dark, splendid, wide-reaching cedars.

The sun sank behind the rim of the mountain wall throwing a massive shadow across the valley. Arne kept glancing worriedly at Sone to see if the effect of the temperwort was wearing off, but he walked on, seeming no different. It grew duskier, a few fireflies winked in the foliage, and the road was a pale ribbon in the dark grass.

Frey said, suddenly, "Do you smell it?"

It was sweet woodsmoke. Arne had noticed it a moment before she spoke.

They hurried their steps. And now, for the first time, Sone spoke. His voice was choked as if his tongue was swollen.

"It won't do any good, you know," he said.

"Never mind, Sone," said Arne. "We'll be there, soon, and everything will be all right." *I hope,* he added to himself.

"You're a fool," Sone mumbled.

He lurched against Arne who, taken unawares, staggered sideways into the grass. Sone grunted, and suddenly his hands were free; he had been working at his bonds for some time and had loosened the bowstring. He whipped out his flint dagger and slashed at Arne. He could not quite reach him and the point only scratched Arne's arm from shoulder to elbow, drawing beads of blood.

Arne recovered his balance. He had been carrying Sone's ax, and he used the helve like a club, striking at Sone's hand, trying to disarm him. But Sone leaped back and stood panting, his teeth gleaming in the dusk, looking from Arne to Frey who, at the commotion, had turned and was stringing her bow.

"You two—" he said, in a grating, horrible voice that sounded like rocks grinding together. "You can't know how much I hate you."

Frey had an arrow on the string. "Sone," she said, "drop your knife. I can't kill you, but I can shoot you in the arm or the leg."

It was clear she meant it. At the same time, a voice called out of the gathering darkness, "Who's there?"

"Hurry!" cried Frey. "We need help."

Arne saw the flash of Sone's eyes as he turned his head. He saw his hand fly up holding the dagger.

"No, Sone!" he shouted, guessing the other's intention as a swell of passion rose in his mind with a force that shook him.

On that crest, Sone threw back his head and gave a piercing cry, full of suffering, that echoed and reechoed among the hills. He struck down, driving the dagger into his chest. His howl ended in a grunt. He sank to his knees and toppled forward, at peace at last.

Five

The village of potters was a cheerful, busy place, too busy to spare more than half an hour next morning to bury Sone, too cheerful to drop a tear for him. "He came to the end of his time," said Dojin, the man who had hailed Arne and Frey in the dusk, and had led them to Ten Bamboos when he had made sure there was no life left in Sone. "He has reckoned up everything and if, as you tell us, he has killed Human Beings, he has restored the Balance by killing himself."

"That's true," said Frey. "Nevertheless, I can't stop feeling sorry for him."

"No doubt he is grateful, wherever he is," said Dojin, his fat-cheeked face solemn. "As for us, we have to watch the kilns."

It was not hardheartedness. The truth was that the potters' work never seemed to be done. When they were not digging clay from the pits in the side of the hill, they were throwing pots or making platters and boxes; when they were not stoking the fires that heated the kilns, they were stacking pots to be baked or taking them out; when they were not glazing, they were making drawings and plans for new shapes. They talked, ate and slept pottery, and at the same time they farmed their fields, milked their goats, set snares for small game, fished in the stream and kept up somehow with the endless woodcutting that had to be done to feed the fires of the kilns. Yet they still found time for fun, and at night there always seemed to be chattering, laughter and singing in someone's house, even while other people worked on.

There was one person in the village whose life followed a slightly different pattern. That was the painter, Juda. Part of his time was spent designing decorations for pots, or painting them, but a good part went into the painting of pictures that served no purpose but to be looked at. Arne and Frey went to visit him in his studio that day after the noon meal.

His house, like that of the others, was long and low with wide eaves and a roof of straw thatch, but it was set a little apart on a rounded knoll near the grove of old bamboos which gave the village its name. The central room was quite large and had a sliding wooden wall, now pushed open, which looked toward the river. Here they found Juda sitting before a low table on which were spread sheets of mulberry-bark paper, pots of ink and water, and dozens of brushes of all sizes from tiny ones made of only two or three rabbit hairs to huge, fat ones as big as a man's arm.

He was short, like most of the potters, but sturdily built, with a round, flat face and a flat, pug nose, and when he smiled his face took on an irresistibly comical expression. But his eyes were sad, even somber. When Arne and Frey arrived, he was painting a tree with smooth, even swoops of the brush. They stood politely silent until he looked up at them.

"I saw an album of your pictures when the Sea Riders came to our village," Arne said. "I thought that a man who could paint so beautifully must be worth seeing."

"You were right," Juda said. With the point of the brush, he touched the paper lightly and quickly. Leaves appeared on the gnarled branch he had drawn. "It's not every day you will see anyone as ugly as I am, who paints so well. Where is your village?"

"It's called Strand, and it lies far from here, up the coast," said Arne. "I am Arne, and this is my friend, Frey."

Juda looked at him in surprise. "And you have really come all this way just to see me?"

"Well, er, not *just* . . ." Arne's voice trailed off and he looked at Frey in embarrassment, caught in the trap of his own politeness.

She said, "We don't mean to be discourteous. Arne only meant that since we had to come this way we wanted to see you as well." She went on to explain their errands.

Juda laid down his brush. "I am complimented that you should have taken the time to come," he said, "and ashamed to have kept you standing so long. Please sit down."

There were thick pillows stuffed with sweet rushes on the floor. Juda went to a polished wooden sideboard and took down a slender pitcher and three small cups, all in a crackled white glaze painted with clusters of bamboo leaves. He poured out an amber liquid with a spicy scent.

"Our plum wine," said he. "Almost as good as our pottery, we think."

They sipped. It had a bitter overtone which set off its sweetness.

"And so you must have your ax repaired," Juda said. "As you see, most of us wear no axes, and even those who do rarely have the chance to use them against *crom*. They do not often come over the cliffs. But you must be careful when you have crossed the pass, for the forests around The Pale Woman are full of them, and I don't think you will get to Osan's house without seeing some."

"Is it hard to get to Osan's? And can you show us the pass?" Arne asked.

"Yes to both." Juda held up his cup and eyed it, turning it in his hand. "Do you like these cups? They were made by an old friend of mine, many years ago."

Arne felt a tug of impatience, but examined his own cup. The surface was like broken eggshell against which the delicate dark green of the painted leaves seemed to flicker.

"They're lovely," said Frey.

"Yes," Juda said. He was sitting facing the open wall, and he pointed to the bamboo grove which could just be seen to the right. "Do you see how the leaves shiver in the breeze? My friend, Karasu, sitting here one day, asked me to paint them so that she could have the design for a set of cups she was making, these cups."

Arne said, "We haven't anything quite so fine in our village."

As he said it, a wave of terrible yearning for home swept over him. He blinked away the moisture that filled his eyes, and looked at Frey. She nodded, and her hand reached for his.

Juda said, "But no doubt you have other things, fine in their own way. I know you are eager to go. Nevertheless, on your journey, you will be given heart by remembering a peaceful moment admiring a cup, tasting wine and thinking of what is past."

He set down the cup and rose. He slid aside the panel of the rear wall and motioned to them to join him. On that side of the house there was a garden of rocks overgrown with miniature flowers and moss, among which stood a few bent mulberry trees like meditating gardeners. The ground tilted to a thick fringe of pines and spruces, and beyond them rose the craggy wall of rock. Foreshortened as it was by nearness, it did not look high but it was almost vertical.

"That is the way you must go," said Juda. "Look along it to the right. Do you see that place where a darker line appears? There you will find a fissure; it is the only place up which you can climb."

Arne sucked air in between his teeth. "It certainly doesn't look easy. But if it's the only way, we'll have to do it."

"We had better start, then," said Frey. "The longer we put it off, the harder it will get."

She turned to Juda. "Thank you for giving us that moment."

He smiled, and went to the sideboard again. Opening a door in the lower part, he fumbled about on the shelves and then brought out a little book which he gave to Frey.

It was no bigger than her hand, its covers made of thin wooden boards polished to show the grain. She opened it and Arne looked at it with her. There were only eight pages, but on each was a tiny painting, marvelously done, of mountains, waterfalls and trees, wreathed with mist and set with houses among which people worked at kilns or in fields.

"Don't thank me," Juda said, hastily. "I have done too many pictures over the years. I'm glad to get rid of it."

They embraced him as if he were an elder brother, and left. They looked back from the path, and he was already sitting before his table, brush in hand.

They returned to Dojin's house, where they had lodged, and gathered their belongings. Dojin and his wife were at work in an open shed, glazing pots, and they stopped long enough to make sure their young son had filled the travelers' packs with food and their leather bottles with water. Having assured themselves of that they wasted no more time but gave the two a cheerful good-bye and went back to their labor.

Arne and Frey plodded uphill, past long kilns built on the incline, past the orchards where apples, plums and pears were ripening, and at last entered the woods. They walked among the gray-green boles of pines with bark like lizard skin. The tang of resin filled their nostrils. The air was hot but dry and invigorating, and it buzzed with the little sawmills of the cicadas.

They bore to the right and came out of the woodland after a time, at the base of the cliff. It soared up so straight that it seemed to overhang them, and instinctively they

cowered away from it as they walked, as if it would topple
on them. They followed its skirts, picking their way among
sharp slabs which had split off and fallen. A little way on,
they saw the fissure opening before them. From Juda's
house it had seemed no more than a slit, but in fact its base
would have held his house with room for the garden. Its
inner side, jagged and offering many handholds, slanted
away from them. They put their sandals in their packs,
checked over their gear, tightening all straps and thongs,
and began to climb.

As they ascended, the fissure narrowed and bent to one
side so that soon they were climbing one face of it. The
handholds were fewer and sometimes they clung, it seemed,
by their nails and will power alone, searching for the next
place to put their fingers and toes. Frey was in the lead,
Arne below since he was the stronger of the two, in a kind
of desperate hope that if she fell he might be able to hold
her, although both knew in their hearts that if she fell they
would go down together. They crept upward like snails
for an endless time. The fissure grew still smaller, and there
came a deep crack, deep enough so that they could plant
their feet in it with their backs against the opposite wall,
and rest. Looking up, they saw that the outer faces of the
fissure came together leaving only a chimney rising through
the rock and opening far above to show whitish sky.

They went up it inch by inch, bracing their feet against
one side, their backs against the other. They emerged on a
shelf wide enough so that they could lie down, side by side,
nearly exhausted. The sky was filled with milky cloud, reddened by the last of the sun on the other side of the cliff

wall. Looking down, they saw that the valley from which they had come was already lost in night.

And looking up, they saw that the cliff wall continued above them, not so sheer, slanting backward and offering in its flawed and broken front a way to ascend, but far too high to attempt in the dark. When they had recovered their strength, they opened their packs and got out food. They were so tired that they had to force themselves to eat, and as they did so it began to drizzle, thin, cold and penetrating.

Clasped in each other's arms, they passed a night of little sleep. A wind sprang up chilling them to the heart. They chafed each other's limbs to keep warm, but could not dry themselves or escape from the rain which blew in upon them. Morning found them almost as weary as the night before, themselves and all their belongings wet through. But the clouds had broken and the rim of the sun was appearing over the far hills on their left. Its rays gave them new strength. They ate with appetite and turned to the climb again.

The rock was still wet, and consequently slippery, but they moved on, sometimes having to go some distance to one side or the other following a flaw, but being able to rest now and then by lying flat against the sloping face, clinging on like flies. The sun grew hotter and they could feel themselves steaming in it. Soon, between exertion and the growing heat they were wet through again, but this time with sweat.

It was well past noon when they reached a shelf which allowed them to stand erect with their faces to the rock and edge upward, foot by foot, to the last face, inclined like a gentle roof up which they ran. They were on the top and they stood breathing hard, gazing at the spectacular view on either side. They could see, now, why this place, high as it was and difficult of achievement, was still the only way over.

It was as if the earth had split apart along a line curving from southeast to northwest, and the part to the south had risen high above the other. The top of the pass was the lowest part of it. To right and left ran the unscalable line of the rocky precipice and then dropped away slowly into wooded crests in the hazy distance. Somewhere along the left hand end lay the road they had departed from, the road from Havens to Red Stones, and looking around the sweep of horizon behind them and to the left they could see the glinting of the sea. Ahead of them, on the other side of the pass, the risen land slid downward into a forest, among the green of which were the polished surfaces of lakes or ponds. Far away, in the haze, a line of silver appeared: the sea again. Ranked to the south, beyond the treetops, were curiously-shaped, low mountains, their blue sides like steps going to flattened tops. One, taller than the rest, showed a bare summit of faintly shining rock, pallid against the sky.

"The Pale Woman," said Frey. "It must be."

"Do you remember the eightsome dance-poem by Bakko, the one in which he says farewell to his love?"

> *The lamp burns low and dies.*
> *Smoke hangs on the morning air*
> *And fades like memory,*

quoted Frey.

"Yes. 'But wait for me—' that part. Well, The Pale Woman will have to wait for me. I'm going to eat."

"Oh, Arne! Shame on you, to remember that poem only for the sake of your stomach."

"Well, you needn't eat," Arne said, sitting down and pulling open the strings of his knapsack. "You can recite as much as you like."

"And let you guzzle down most of the food? Not a chance."

She sat beside him and they devoured the rest of the shortbread, the cold roasted mountain partridge, the dried fruit and goat's milk cheese Dojin's son had given them. They felt very lighthearted after the long climb and everything now seemed easy. They put their sandals on again and looked over their gear. Their leather knapsacks and belt pouches had kept out the wet, their bowstrings and ax heads had been well waxed and had not suffered. They stood up, refreshed and ready, and started the much easier climb down to the forest.

Late afternoon found them among giant maples and oaks, so big that their tangled branches made an artificial evening below. Fat, blue-gray squirrels lived here in profusion and they shot two for their dinner. They found a hollow tree and with Frey's ax widened the opening at the base enough so that they could take shelter inside. By the light of a small fire they looked at Juda's book, and talked of their adventures and of home, and found, as he had said, that the memory heartened them. Before sunrise, they were up and had eaten, and as the first few probing fingers of sunlight came slanting between the tree trunks to give them their direction, they set out again, southward.

They had come after an hour or so to broken ground, where the trees were further apart and jags of limestone burst upward like knees or elbows frilled with bracken. Frey, leading as usual, lifted a warning hand and pointed. Arne saw what appeared to be a hump of blue earth before one such point made of two rocks leaning together like hands joined in prayer. Even as he looked, he had an arrow on the string of his bent bow, for the hump moved and shifted and became blue fur striped with pale gray.

It was a big cat. It had its back to them and was fishing for something with one paw between the rocks. Its haunches were high, its stub of a tail twitching. It was bigger than any cat they had ever seen. The infrequent ones which came into the hunting territory of Strand and were killed by parties of determined trackers stood half as high as a man at the shoulder and might weigh eighty or ninety pounds, but this one was twice that size. It whirled almost as soon as they saw it, crouching back against the rocks. Its head with the wide, silky ruff was almost on a level with Frey's.

It opened its mouth and hissed menacingly, showing teeth like daggers, the incisors as long as Arne's fingers. Arne felt no fear, only admiration. It was as beautiful as it was deadly, with its shining fur, its spreading ruff, its round golden eyes. It was healthy, proud, quick, full of life.

"Can we get away?" Frey said, softly.

"I don't think so. It's hunting, it's got something in among the rocks. Be careful, it's planning to charge."

The cat, mouth half open, head and shoulders low, advanced a step or two toward them. They could see the muscles on its back grow tense beneath the striped hide.

"Forgive us," Arne said to it. "We shall have to kill you for our own sakes."

At the same time, he began walking to the right while Frey walked to the left. They moved decisively and swiftly, and their abrupt separation made the cat pause for an instant, turning its head from one to the other, making up its mind which to attack. That instant was enough. Their arrows sped almost together and struck it, Frey's in the eye, Arne's in the chest, sinking deeply in at that short range. It sprang at him with a yowl, and as it raised itself he shot again and hit it in the throat. It fell in midair and lay still, blood spotting the blue fur.

They walked cautiously nearer, knowing quite well that a dying animal can, in its death spasm, kill a hunter. As they looked at it in sorrow a slight noise made them turn their heads. From the opening between the rocks at which the cat had been pawing, a *crom* emerged.

It was young, and the hair on its face and body was sparse, giving it a nearly human appearance. It was a female, not as old as Frey and not her height. Its left arm had been torn by the cat and it held that wrist in its other hand; it looked frightened and defenseless.

Frey dropped her bow and reached for her ax, but uncertainly. Arne caught her hand.

"No," he said.

The *crom* stared at them, cowering in anticipation of a blow. It said, "Uh—uh—" and then with difficulty, shaping its lips, "No, no," and painfully lifted its hurt arm with its right hand.

"It can talk," Frey said, with a shudder, between fascination and disgust.

"Melot has told me that they know some words," said Arne.

He went up to the *crom,* looking into its face in a bemused way. His eyes held those of the creature for a moment, and then it turned its head away.

"Look at me," Arne said. "Can you understand?"

It peered at him from under its overhanging brows, and looked down again, mumbling, "Not—hurt me." Its manner reminded Arne, with a pang, of Sone. Then it said, "Home, home," and its voice broke. To their astonishment, tears fell glittering from its eyes.

Arne recoiled before the unexpected, almost shameful sight of the thing weeping like a Human Being.

"Go home, then," he said, harshly. "Hurry. Go, or we'll kill you."

It waited no longer. Without another word, without a look, it sprang between Arne and Frey and ran off swiftly, vanishing between the trees, leaving a little pool of blood where it had been standing.

"If it could talk, it might have said thank you," Frey said. She raised her shoulders delicately, shivering. "Ugh! I'd sooner have the cat talk to me."

"Yes, but tell me the truth," Arne said, gravely. "Could you have killed it? It was so helpless."

Frey bit her lip. "When they grow up they're anything but helpless. Still, maybe not, not when it was wounded, not in cold blood."

She went and got her bow, stooping to examine the cat. It was dead. "What about this?" she said. "Shall we skin it?"

"We can't spare the time."

"It seems a waste."

"I know, but if there are *crom* around it's better not to be burdened."

Before they set out again, Frey found a tree with branches sweeping low to the ground. She swung lightly into it and made her way nearly to the top. In spite of the thick foliage, she was able to get a glimpse of The Pale Woman, now looming close, less than a half day's journey away. The flattened summit cast back the daylight; the rock up there was so light colored as to make her think it might be covered with snow, but the mountain was not high enough for that. She climbed down again and told Arne what she had seen.

"We can be there in a couple of hours, I think," she said.

"I wonder where Osan's house is."

"The map showed only that it was high on the shoulder of the sunrise side."

"We'll try that way first, then."

The forest had broken into glades interspersed with fields of wild timothy and clover, and ponds where ducks flew splashing up as the two appeared. With more open land, The Pale Woman came into full view, its sides grassy and dotted only sparsely with stunted junipers, a smooth and easy climb, Arne thought. They met no real obstacles and had no sign of *crom,* and by late morning, the sun standing almost overhead, they found themselves in a valley with hills on both sides of them and The Pale Woman before them closing off the end. Bushes grew there of a kind they did not know, the leaves blue-green on top and yellow-green below so that they shimmered light and dark in every breeze. They were covered with small, pure white berries, too waxy to be edible. There were also some smooth-trunked trees, a kind of beech Arne thought, but low and twisted like cypresses. Picking their way among the bushes they approached their goal.

"Shall we start upward?" Frey asked.

"Let's—" Arne began, and never finished, for two short, sharp, explosive sounds interrupted him.

They both spun around, bows half drawn, only to stare incredulously at the animal which had made the noise. It was like nothing they had ever seen before. It was large, about half the size of the cat they had killed. Its pelt was wiry and short, spotted black and brown. It was heavy in the chest, but long-legged and light in the hindquarters like a runner, and it had a thin, short tail which switched from side to side in an eager sort of way. In spite of its sharp teeth it did not look unfriendly; indeed, its pointed muzzle and pricked ears gave it an inquisitive appearance, and its light hazel eyes were filled with good-humored intelligence.

Once again, it uttered its convulsive cry. As it did so, Arne felt what he could only describe as a creeping in his mind. It was like the prickling of his scalp when he was alarmed, only deep in his brain, a kind of tickling and crawling of the imagination so outrageously strange that he cried out wordlessly and dropped his bow. Clearly, Frey felt nothing, for she stared at him in alarm.

A silent voice, like a voice heard in a dream, said inside his head: *Not. Fear. Not fear. Fear not.*

And then, more distinctly, *Don't be afraid.*

The beast was sitting on its haunches, its tongue lolling out. It looked as if it were grinning.

Arne said, stammering, "Who are you? What do you want?"

The voice in his mind said, *I am Osan.*

"What is happening?" Frey cried.

"This creature is Osan," Arne said. "I can't believe—it's talking to me in my mind."

No, said the silent voice, becoming clearer and more intelligible. *This creature is Dag. I am Osan. I am speaking to you through it—through its brain.*

In a way, this was even stranger than if the beast itself had really been Osan.

Arne said, "If you—I mean, how—what do you—?"

There was no sound of laughter, but an effervescence of amusement filled his mind. Then the voice said, *Follow Dag. He will bring you to me.*

With that, the beast jumped up and ran off a little way, stopping to see if they were coming.

"Somehow," Arne explained to Frey, "Osan spoke to me through that animal. She wants us to follow it."

He picked up his bow and they set off. They had gone no more than a hundred paces when Dag stopped short and began barking furiously. It ran back toward them, spun around to face the hills on their right, and barked again, so urgently that its hind legs bent under it like springs.

Down the hillside came a band of *crom,* half a dozen of them perhaps. They were led by a huge old male, its body eerily covered with silvery-white hair, a short club in each of its hands.

Dag was already disappearing among the bushes. "Don't wait!" Arne cried, to Frey. "Don't try to fight—too many of them. Run!"

She bounded off at once. Arne glanced back at the *crom* and saw the leader halt. *Are they afraid to attack?* he thought, and waited just for a breath, to see.

The leader drew back its arm and hurled one of the clubs. End over end it came on the very instant of Arne's hesitation, too fast, too sudden to escape.

Arne fell into blackness.

Six

There was a soft chattering all around him. His head ached, and he rolled over on his side and opened his eyes. A hand was beneath his shoulders and someone helped him to sit up.

He looked into the face of a *crom,* an elderly female with no hair to speak of on her face, whose expression, amused and concerned, reminded him of Old Matte as she had looked when she had painted the symbol of the ax on his throat so long ago, at his initiation. It made him homesick.

She had a large leaf, pinned together with splinters of wood to make a rude cup, and full of water. She held it to his lips and said, "Take."

He did so, bending forward and grimacing at the pain in his skull. Then he sank back, supporting himself on his hands.

All his belongings except his belt pouch were gone. He was in a glade of tall, slender birches and aspens, and he could hear a brook chuckling not far off. Among the trees, elderberries grew thickly and several *crom* were moving about, gathering the clusters of dark berries and breaking shelving funguses from the birches. They were females who were harvesting, dropping what they picked into large baskets woven of osiers. It was their voices Arne had heard, they were talking softly among themselves in words he could not understand. Little ones, hairless except for their long, tousled manes, ran about, helped with the gleaning, or fought with each other. They could hardly be distinguished from Human Beings, Arne thought muzzily. There were a few males, as well, two of them using sharp stones to fashion clubs, holding the ends of sticks between their toes and shaving away splinters almost as Human Beings might shape an ax handle. Another male was searching the undergrowth for snails, collecting them in a bucket made of birchbark. They all looked peaceable enough. Their smell, however, rank and dirty, revolted him.

Arne saw the big, white-haired leader of the band seated on the ground some distance off, his eyes closed. A young female knelt beside him, scratching his head with one hand. Her other arm was clotted with dried blood, and as she glanced up her eyes met Arne's and he recognized her. She was the one he and Frey had let go.

His lip curled. It was she, then, who had betrayed him. She must have run straight back and warned the band that there were strangers about. She still watched him, and he spat on the ground in disgust.

To his surprise, she covered her mouth with her hand and with a look of distress shook her head vehemently. Did she mean to convey that she had said nothing after all? He found that hard to believe, and yet that was certainly how it appeared.

He had no more time to think of it, for the leader had opened his eyes when the scratching stopped, and had noticed him. He gave a shout and the old crone hauled Arne to his feet and half led, half dragged him over.

On the grass beside the white-haired one lay Arne's knapsack, its contents strewn about, along with his flint knife, his bow and quiver, and his ax. He eyed the ax, wondering if he could make a grab for it and somehow fight his way out. He gave up the idea as the white-haired *crom* stood up between him and his belongings. He was nearly a head taller than Arne, and he looked down at him with bloodshot eyes and growled menacingly. Arne shrank back.

This seemed to please the leader. Bending so that his face was close to Arne's, he said, "I eat you."

Arne's flesh crept in horror, and he could not keep from showing his dismay. The white-haired one's mouth opened crookedly, and he began to make a loud, rhythmic noise.

Abruptly Arne realized that he was laughing. This was even more of a shock than the threat had been. Before he could know how to take it, the other lost interest in him, gave him a shove of dismissal and turned his back. Arne waited uncertainly and then walked away. There seemed no reason he should not simply leave the band.

He found the reason when he got to the nearest large tree. A bandy-legged male with black hair stepped out from behind it and seizing him by the arm whirled him around and sent him sprawling headlong. He followed this up by kicking him once or twice, and then went back to his sentry duty.

For what remained of the long summer afternoon, Arne waited to be eaten. No one, however, paid much attention to him except for a few of the cubs who first stared at him in fear and then, from a distance, threw stones or pieces of fungus at him until the old female ran at them with a stick and drove them away. She hovered near him, keeping an eye on him after his abortive attempt to escape, and he had no doubt she would call for help if he tried again. The *crom* had a language of their own which sounded to Arne as senseless as the chattering of sparrows, and which was spoken, it seemed, mainly among the females—at least, he heard nothing from the males beyond an occasional monosyllable. Yet they could, he knew, speak a few words of Human speech and he wondered whether their own tongue contained true words or consisted only of the sounds animals might make to soothe or threaten or warn. They seemed to hang midway between human and animal. As the females twittered to one another, dropping their berries into the baskets, they had a most human air, then, suddenly, one would screech what might have been curses at another who had pushed in ahead of her or snatched a particularly large bunch of berries, and there would be clawing and slapping. Once the leader knocked a young one out of his way with a careless blow of the hand. No Human in Strand would have done such a thing. Arne wondered what thoughts went through their shaggy heads, and whether there was any glimmer of imagination behind those small, deep-sunken eyes.

He watched the white-haired one, not only with apprehension but to see if he would leave the ax unguarded. Even with part of its blade curled back it was a formidable weapon, and he thought: *a quick rush, snatch it up, a blow, and while the* crom *are disorganized by the death of their leader, run off into the woods. And then?* He told himself over and over that Frey must have gotten away for there was no sign of anything belonging to her and surely if they had killed her they would have brought back her ax, if nothing else? Where had she gone? Could he rejoin her? Had she climbed The Pale Woman? Had she met that strange creature, Dag, and made her way with it to Osan? Perhaps Osan would know a way to rescue Arne, in which case he might do better to stay where he was and wait. *Yes,* he told himself, *stay and be killed by some whim of these soulless things who hardly seem to know their own minds from moment to moment!* He thought not. He must do something, but the white-haired one never moved far from the ax and bow, and the old female kept her eye on Arne even as she combed her hair with her fingers or looked for grubs under stones.

The sun was low when two more males appeared, bringing a few squirrels and a blue-furred opossum. The *crom* had no art of making flint tools. Their weapons were their short clubs, and pebbles which they threw with great accuracy, and their tools were stones smashed with rocks to make sharp edges which they used in a variety of ways. With such fragments, they skinned and cut up the game. They shared it out, along with berries and snails, the leader eating first and after him the other males, and lastly the females and young; this order of precedence emphasized, for Arne, their inhuman quality. The leader threw a bit of raw meat to Arne who ate it hungrily. It was all he got.

It was almost dark by the time they had finished, and the band began settling down for the night. *Now,* Arne said to himself, *a chance might come.* Surely, they could not watch him all night long? His hope was dashed almost at once. The black-haired male who had stopped him leaving grabbed his arm and dragged him to a tree. He forced Arne to sit down at its base and then, with Arne's own bowstrings, first lashed his wrists behind his back and then tied them to the tree trunk.

Arne sat in miserable discomfort while the *crom* curled up on the ground in twos and threes, the young ones cuddled close to them. In the darkness, he could hear them clucking softly; then they were quiet. He leaned his shoulders back against the tree to rest, meaning to try to get loose somehow as soon as he was sure they were all sound asleep, but he had had a long and active day. His eyes closed in spite of himself, and he dozed off.

He was brought wide awake by a touch on his wrists. His eyes snapped open and he found that the moon had risen, a sharp half-moon above the lacy foliage. By its light he could see what he had already learned from smell and touch, that someone was bending close to him, working at his bonds. It was the young female with the wounded arm, and·an instant later she had cut through the bowstrings with the undamaged part of his ax blade.

As he drew his hands apart and began to rub his wrists, wincing against the pain of the returning circulation, she drew away and with a nervous gesture held out the ax to him. He took it, in wonderment. She cupped her hand over her mouth, meaning him to be silent, and he nodded to show he understood. She pointed to the forest but still he sat watching her, more surprised by her actions than by anything he had seen so far.

She mistook his hesitation and pointed again, more emphatically. He bent forward and patted her cheek, not knowing how else to thank her. Her eyes reflected the moonlight and he could not tell what emotion was in them or if, indeed, there was any. He got up and slipped off among the trees, using all his hunter's skill to move as noiselessly as a deer.

He had not gone five hundred paces from the sleeping camp when a figure stepped out in front of him and spoke his name, softly.

"Frey!" he said, and they were in each other's arms.

"Don't speak here," she whispered, close to his ear. "Follow me."

She led him through the silver-dappled woods at a light, swift trot, and into the gloom of a high hill. She stopped, at last, before a darker blot among the shadows.

"We can hide here," she said.

He squinted uneasily into the low cave mouth. "We may be trapped inside."

"Perhaps. But it goes a long way in. We can defend ourselves more easily in there than in the open."

"How did you—?"

"They didn't follow me, and when they carried you away with them I tracked them to their camp. I watched for a while from a tree branch and saw that you couldn't get away, so I decided to wait until nightfall. I explored a bit, to see if I could decide which way we had better go, and found this cave. This is the back of the hill down which they came to attack us. Over there, on the other side, is The Pale Woman. If they don't follow us, we can climb this hill tomorrow and make our way up onto the mountain. I cut some pine boughs for us to use as torches in the cave. Then I went back to the camp, to watch. I had to keep out of the way of the two who were hunting. I wanted to wait until moonrise so that I could be sure of finding you, but I—I dozed off. Still, it wasn't too late."

"You were always a better planner than I," Arne said, with admiration.

"I told you a long time ago you needed someone to look after you," she smiled.

"You saw the young *crom* set me free?"

"Yes. I could not guess at first what she was after when she crept toward you with the ax. I didn't dare move for fear of waking them all, but I had an arrow on the string, ready for her. However, I could see almost at once that she was cutting you free. What made her do it?"

"I think," Arne said, "she was grateful."

Frey raised her eyebrows. "Grateful? A *crom?*"

"Yes, I think so. For letting her go when we killed the cat. What other reason?"

She shrugged. "Who knows why they do what they do?"

He let the matter drop. "Let's look at this cave of yours. Where are the torches?"

"Just inside."

Groping, they found them, eight longish pieces of pine. She had sliced into the bark at the end of each, peeling it back but leaving it attached so that it would flame up more readily. With a flint arrowhead and the back of an ax they struck sparks and got some bits of tinder smoldering, blew up a small blaze and lighted one of the torches from it.

As soon as he had entered, holding the torch high, Arne was captured by an almost childish delight in caves and forgot everything in his wish to explore. It was worth exploring. The rocky walls sparkled with mica, and here and there veins of quartz with enormous crystals shot out diamond gleams in the smoky light and faded again. The passage wound inward for a long way and then opened into a much larger chamber which looked as though some vast bubble of gas had formed in it and burst, pushing the walls apart, leaving a rounded roof from which hung fingers of translucent, green stone. From the far end another passage opened, twisting upwards between walls striped in colored layers like an extravagant geological birthday cake.

"Shall we—?" Arne was beginning, when a distant noise reached them, a prolonged howling, faint as yet.

"They've discovered you're gone. They're on our trail," said Frey.

"Right. This is no good, this chamber. It's too big. Let's go on into that passage opposite. It's smaller, and we can hold them off there. Or perhaps there's another way out."

They entered the striped passage and after a little distance had to squeeze between projecting points of rock. Beyond, the way was narrower and led them back and forth, as if water had streamed through, forcing its way past obstacles, surging first one way and then another.

"It goes upward," Frey said, rubbing a scratch on her shoulder. "Maybe you're right, maybe there is another way out up above."

Arne grunted. "I wonder if they guessed she cut the cords," he muttered. "Maybe they'll know I couldn't have taken the ax and done it myself."

"They won't know anything," said Frey. "They don't think."

"No, perhaps not. Or maybe they'll remember that you were with me and got away."

"It's no good worrying about it. Go on. My eyes are running so from the torch that I can barely see. Perhaps there's a little more space further along that'll let some of the smoke out."

He pushed on, and after a bit the passage did, in fact, grow larger. They stepped forward into a tunnel which ran almost but not quite level at a sharp angle to the way they had been going. Arne raised the torch, which was about half burned away. This new passage was curiously regular, its walls and roof of dark featureless stone, broken and fallen here and there but giving the impression, almost, of having been shaped by men rather than nature.

Arne glanced at the flame. It bent very slightly to the left. "What air there is is moving from the right," he said. "And it slants a little upward that way, so let's try it."

They made their way along the tunnel for an interminable time. Twice they had to light a fresh torch. The third was nearly gone when they came to a place where the roof had collapsed, leaving a mass of rubble and large stones. Above their heads gaped an opening. They climbed the heap with difficulty, and Arne thrust the torch up. There was another cave there. He scrambled into it with Frey at his heels, lighted another torch from the old one and looked about.

Thrill after thrill ran through him. The hair on the back of his neck rose. "This place is—" he said, and could not continue.

Before them was a wall of polished stone with part of an archway still standing in it. Above the archway were cut symbols, so regular that they could only be the letters of some unimaginable alphabet:

G R A N D   C E N T R . . T E R M I . . .
T o   U p p e . . . v e l

Frey pressed close to him, as overwhelmed as he was. "What is it?" she said. "What does it mean?"

"It was a house. Something like a house. It must have belonged to—" He fell silent, unable to guess.

"How could it come to be buried here, under The Pale Woman?"

"I don't know. I can't guess. But it's old . . ."

Drawn almost against his will, he approached the archway. There were stairs in it, rising into the darkness.

"Should we?" said Frey. "I'm frightened."

"You?" he said. "*You* frightened? Not you, Frey."

"All right. But hold my hand."

The stairs were cracked and crumbling but enough of them remained so that the ascent was not too difficult.

They turned left and left again and emerged in a small cavern formed by great, smooth slabs of stone. Frey touched one edge, too right-angled to be natural and showing traces of the same polishing. The cavern led to another, and another, a whole chain of them, in places so low that the two had to crawl on hands and knees, in other places high and vaulted so that the clink of one stone against another underfoot echoed above them. Arne watched his torch and followed the tiny flicker that showed a current of air still coming from somewhere above.

They came to another stair, partly choked by stone that appeared to have been ground to powder. They were able to get past, coughing in the dust, and climbed on over blocks partly splintered by the weight of others. Once, they saw, half buried in stone, some large pieces of transparent stuff which flashed back a reflection of the torch and yet, when they looked more closely, let them see the rock beneath it. Arne was reminded of the disk Weikar had held in his eye—it seemed a lifetime ago. Another time they saw the remains of a column, perfectly straight and square, made, it seemed, of rust like an ax that had been left to lie in the rain. It was held in place by hard-packed earth around it.

They went upward and upward, sometimes following ruined stairs, sometimes clambering over rocks or crawling through crevices where Arne first thrust the torch through and then forced his body after it. They were scratched in a dozen places and Frey limped from a bruised ankle. She had taken off her knapsack to prevent it from catching on projections, and carried it and her bow and quiver; Arne had both axes.

They lighted their last torch, and by its yellow resinous flame looked at each other.

"Are you still afraid?" Arne asked.

"Not any more," she replied, in her clear voice. "If we die, we die. Give me a kiss."

He embraced her. "Perhaps we shouldn't have tried this," he said, "but I'm glad I saw it."

"So am I. I will be even gladder if we can remind each other about it a year from now."

They laughed together and turned to the ascent once more.

The torch burned lower and lower and still they climbed. Arne felt the weight of earth and stone pressing upon him, growing more and more unendurable, and worse yet the sense of utter dark just outside the flickering flame. And then the time came when the torch could no longer be held. He dropped the last bit of wood, licking his hand where it had been scorched. The fire died and there remained only a glow and a few sparks.

He turned to Frey—and stood staring. Her face emerged grayly out of the blackness. In the moment it took for him to understand, she said, "I can see you. There's light coming from somewhere."

As she spoke, he felt a small but steady current of air brush his cheek. The light came from a hole a little way above them. They scrambled up the side of a tilted slab to come to it. It was large enough for them to squeeze

through, and when they had done so they stood up hope-
fully.

They were at the base of a crack three or four times
Arne's height, and as they looked at it their hearts sank. It
was not much wider than his hand, as if the stone had been
sliced into by a gigantic sword. They put their faces close
to it, Frey stooping so that Arne could look over her head.
They could see, now, how high they had climbed. They
were inside The Pale Woman, somewhere on that side
looking into the valley where they had met Dag. The
forest spread out beyond, a carpet of green, and in the
melting distance the land rose toward that far curtain of
cliffs where the pass overlooked the potters' village. Just
outside the crack long grasses danced in the breeze. It was
gray dawn and the air was fresh and sweet. They gazed
out longingly.

Arne stepped back and looked up. The reason they
could see the whole length of the crack was that they
stood at the bottom of a kind of pit that had been formed
when there had been some subsidence and the mountainside had split. The walls rose above them, showing fragments of stairs and jumbled masonry, but there was no
way to continue their ascent even if there had been any
purpose in doing so.

He peered out again, pressing his hands on either side
of the crack as if somehow he could push it open. It was
worse to be within sight of freedom and to be locked up
still in prison.

How beautiful the world is! he said to himself. His heart

swelled with pity for Frey, with the love of life, with a passionate yearning to be outside and free.

The solid rock seemed to shift and move; it trembled under his palms. He felt himself falling and caught hold of Frey, and the next moment they had tumbled forward on the steep slope, rolling down in the turf. Bewildered, they clutched at the ground, snatching handfuls of grass, gasping for breath, and at the same time they heard the sharp barking of the beast, Dag.

Seven

Arne, getting on his hands and knees, stared at the crack through which they had spilled. It was wider than the width of his shoulders. Dazed, he stood up and went to inspect it. The stone was immovable, as hard as ever, and the grass grew to its edges as before.

The silent voice of Osan, speaking in his mind, said, *Go with Dag.*

It was hard walking because of the slope, but hand in hand they followed the creature which trotted ahead of them, its tail waving jauntily. They said nothing to each other but neither had any doubt that Osan had somehow liberated them and they wondered with some misgivings what sort of woman she might be.

They were three-quarters of the way up the mountain, and they had to go down a little distance and around a shoulder to the eastern side. There, on a grassy shelf, stood a hut built of stones tightly mortared together, with a flat wooden roof higher at the back than the front so that it was like a cap pulled down over the windows and door. There was a bench beside the door, and on it sat a woman in a brown robe with a cowl thrown back on her shoulders, her hands clasped in her lap. Dag ran up to her, barked once, and sat down looking pleased with himself.

With some trepidation, the two approached the woman and bent their heads courteously. Osan had been looking off into the distance, where the sun was just pushing the edge of its disk over the hills. She turned, reluctantly it seemed, and brought her attention to Arne and Frey.

They were aware, first, of her eyes which were large, almond-shaped, as black as a crow's wing and full of laughter. They were enmeshed in wrinkles, those eyes, and only later did Arne notice that her whole face was a network of tiny wrinkles, barely seeming to crease the skin but covering it like a tracery of spider web. In spite of this, her skin looked fresh, not at all like that of someone so old; it was the color of aged ivory, a deep, soft yellow. She sat perfectly erect but relaxed.

"Good morning," she said, and her voice was husky but lively and full of mirth.

"We thank you," said Arne.

"You are certainly a polite young man," said Osan, "to thank me for a greeting. What's your name, and that of the young woman with you?"

"I am Arne and she is Frey. We are from the village of Strand."

Osan nodded. "Well, Arne and Frey, if you will go into my house you'll find bread and cheese and goat's milk on the table. Bring them out and we'll breakfast."

They did as she bade them, both of them peeping furtively around the hut when they were inside but seeing nothing except a chest, a low bed, a table, and several stools. There was another door in the rear wall but they could not guess why, as the back of the hut was against the mountainside with almost no space between.

Outside again, they sat on the ground at her feet and shared the food, Frey serving Osan, and Arne after a glance at Osan, who nodded, giving some to Dag. They discovered how hungry they were with the first bite, and wasted no time in talking, but when they were done, Osan said, "I cannot believe you came here by chance."

"That is true," Arne said. "I was told to give you this."

He opened his belt pouch and took out the yellow disk engraved with an eye and an ax, which Getsu had given him. Osan weighed it in her palm, thoughtfully.

"It is as well for you that you have this," she said, finally. "I am not always easy to visit, and sometimes the people who come to me without invitation find me cross and disagreeable. I am a dangerous person, you see." She smiled, belying her words, and added, "Now tell me why you were sent to me."

"I fought with a *crom* who had an iron club," said Arne. "It damaged my ax and I decided to go to the village of Red Stones to have it repaired. I was told to visit you on the journey and tell you."

"But you haven't told me," said Osan. "I'm sure Getsu —oh, you needn't look so surprised, I know many names even if I don't leave my mountain very often—Getsu told you to tell me everything that happened. Do so, and leave nothing out, not the smallest thing. Remember, I am a dangerous person."

Arne grinned, not believing this for a minute but anxious to obey because he liked her. Furrowing his brows, he thought carefully back to the day of the raid and then began to tell the story as best he could.

When he had finished, Osan sat for a long time without speaking. The sun had risen, and she stared straight into it, never winking, so that both Arne and Frey began to feel uneasy. At last, she shook herself, looked at them and laughed outright.

"What a pair of nestlings, sitting with your mouths wide open. Are you waiting for a worm?" she said. "Well, I have already filled you with my good bread and cheese and I can spare nothing else. Let me see your ax, Arne."

He held it out, handle foremost. She inspected the dented edge, bringing it close to her eyes, and touched with her thumb the blunted part and the deep nick in the blade. She held it between her hands, edge uppermost, the handle jutting to one side. She smiled at the pair, and fixed her eyes on the metal.

There was a faint stirring along the bright edge as if light were playing there. Not light, but a shimmering of the iron in the sun. Arne bent forward. The metal was moving. It was growing rapidly before his eyes, particle by particle, rearranging itself so that the nick was filled, the folded piece grew thinner and flatter, and finally the whole curve swept smooth and sharp from tip to tip.

"You—you mended it!" Arne gasped.

Frey sat speechless, her face pale.

"Yes," Osan said, "I mended it." She added, drily, "I told you I was a dangerous person."

"Magic," Frey said, in a hushed tone. "But I thought it was only in old tales."

"Not magic," said Osan. "You have forgotten what you were taught. Do you not remember the Tale of Shaping? 'Out of the ending came the beginning.' The Harmony of All Things means that all things are one, stones, birds, water, iron, and men and women, all made from the same substance. A potter takes clay and from it makes many shapes, pots and cups and bowls, but it is all the same clay. I have the power to move that basic substance of which all things are made, to make things rebuild themselves from their own substance, to change their shapes."

Her voice and face had become very grave, even grim. "I am a dancer in the great dance," she said. "When I was young, I danced with others, like you two. Now I dance alone."

They sat quite still, gazing at her in awe. Frey said, timidly, "You have no one to live with you at all?"

Osan's eyes twinkled. "You haven't heard what I have been saying, my dear. You didn't believe me when I said I was dangerous. I am! Do you not see?" She sat up even straighter, if that were possible, and her voice became as hard as the iron of the ax head, and as sharp. "Have you not thought what such power as mine can do? I could hold the world in my hand."

They shrank before her. Arne, struck by a thought, at first did not dare to voice it and then, taking courage, said, "You are not one of us, are you?"

She blinked at him. "One of *you?* What do you mean?"

"You are not a Human Being. You are more than human. Is—is that your house, the ruined house we found under this mountain?"

They expected almost any answer except the one she gave.

"My house—that?" she said, and burst into laughter. "That was a house of the *crom!*"

They were stunned, and then they both began talking at once, "You don't mean that they—" "The *crom* built that?" "But how—?" "—Under the mountain?"

She waved a hand at them until they were silent.

"Well," she said, "I see I must explain or I shall have no peace. I will tell you what few people know, but since you've already been inside the mountain it will not harm you to know the truth about what you've seen.

"The Pale Woman is no mountain but a great building fallen into emptiness and covered by the earth of centuries. If you could climb to the very top you would see that its pale face is neither metal nor stone but some curious, light-colored material which has survived all those years. And these hills around us, too, were buildings, hundreds of them. All that you can see below you, from sunrise to sunset, was once a city, most of it now shaken down flat and the ruins covered up under the forest. People lived there and worked there, more people than you can imagine. Think of it! All this land covered with room upon room, house upon house, and filled with people."

Arne's head ached as he tried to imagine it. Frey said, "And they were all *crom?*"

"They were the ancestors of the *crom*. Not as you see them now, filthy and naked and shambling. They wore clothing and stood erect, and looked like Human Beings. But like the *crom* today, they had no souls. And like the *crom* they did not hesitate to kill one another."

"Yet," Arne said, slowly, "they could build such buildings and such cities. They were not altogether like the *crom* now, who cannot even make flint spears. They must have been—" he groped for an image, frowning "—something like Unfinished People, but grown up."

"Not quite," said Osan. "For they cared nothing for each other's lives. The *crom,* having no souls, will murder each other for a bit of food or for lust, but the ancient people killed each other by hundreds, by thousands, by— such numbers as you cannot guess at. Yet since they had so little regard for life, they also brought more and more of themselves into the world. They knew so much, they must have known also—just as we do—some ways of keeping the Balance so that no more of them would appear than there was room for. But they never thought of it, it seems. They thought of little."

She paused, gathering her thoughts, and went on, "You see, having no souls each of them thought only of itself. They could not imagine how the act of one would affect another, and so each let its own greed, its own desires, have free rein. Tell me, would you in Strand let one person go hungry if the rest had food?"

"Of course not," Frey said. "But then, we are often all hungry together in winter."

"Yes, and that is so with all Human Beings. We all may go hungry at times, but we know that misfortune is easier to bear in company because our souls tell us what others are feeling. We can be hungry and yet find joy. But they mistook the images of things for the things themselves. For instance, each of them thought that if it could only be safe from hunger it would find joy. And so they made gluttons of themselves, stuffing themselves, wasting their food, and when they had more than they could eat, greedily hoarding it, but as they did so, in other places thousands of them starved to death. They thought that if they could be free from work they would find joy, and so they constructed machinery to help them overcome work, but the tending of those machines made work for them without pleasure or satisfaction, a more horrible work than we can guess at.

"They ran after life in so many frantic ways that they never found time to live. They were afraid of death and thought that if they could escape it they would find joy, but death was in everything they did, in their great numbers, in their wastefulness, in their selfishness, in their lack of souls."

"No one can escape death," said Frey. "Did they not know that?"

Osan regarded her pensively. "What they did not know was that even if you could escape death you would have no certainty of finding joy. Where is joy? I do not know, but I know that it does not come from overcoming hunger or work or death, but from overcoming oneself."

Arne stared out over the valley, the forest, the folded hills. "What happened to them?" he said.

Osan shrugged. "We do not know. Perhaps they used up all their treasures, the metals and materials with which they built, and beggared themselves. We have so little iron nowadays that only in a few places such as Red Stones can we find any. Without an abundance, they could not manage for they had to waste more than they used. Perhaps they poisoned their land and water by their thoughtlessness. Perhaps in one of their wars they destroyed their cities—"

"What is a *war?*" Arne put in.

"It is like a raid, but on a much vaster scale. We encourage young people to go raiding, knowing that they must have adventure and danger, but that their souls will keep them from killing each other. But those ancestors of the *crom,* they went in millions to slaughter each other, old and young alike, and for purposes we cannot begin to understand. Perhaps the earth itself revolted against them. We know that there were earthquakes and upheavals which changed the face of things. This mountain, this building, stands on land that has risen. There, to the east, there was once an island a hundred miles long, and to the west, where the swamps lie, was a wide river."

She pointed to the milk jug. "Give me a cup of milk," she said. "So much talking has dried up my throat, which is older than yours."

Arne poured some out for her and as she drank, he said, "Then—are the *crom* all that are left of that time?"

Osan put down her cup. "When the day of that ancient people ended, Human Beings appeared. We do not know for certain how it happened. The power I have is called the *tendo* and there are others who have the same power. We think that people with that power appeared, brought into being by the spirit of Harmony out of the need for keeping the Balance. They awoke the souls in others, as many as they could reach, at first a few, then more and more. So, by degrees, as the ancient people died and their civilization crumbled apart, the Humans received the earth that had been left to them. Some of the others lived on, lurking in forests. They became the *crom*."

It was a great deal to digest, and the two sat turning it over in their minds for a time. At length, Arne said, "I think I understand something. We only kill animals when we must, for food or in self-defense, and we are careful when we do so to keep the Balance. But we kill *crom* whenever we find them, without mercy. It must be because we are afraid they will recover their strength and take away the world once more."

"Just so. Left to themselves, they would breed like mice in a hayloft. They care nothing for killing, and would destroy us all. You have seen them."

"Yes," said Arne, his chin in his hand. "I have seen them. I don't know anyone else who has seen them as I have, except one." He was thinking, as he spoke, of Sone.

Frey said, "And I understand something, too. I can see how terrible it would be if they found out how to make iron clubs. That is why Arne was told to come and tell you what had happened, isn't it? With your power you can stop them."

"I?" Osan raised her brows. "Oh, yes, you are right. I can stop them. I can see to it that the person who gave the *crom* an iron club will not give them another."

"Who was it?" Arne asked eagerly. "Do you know?"

"Yes, I do," she replied. She stood up, and they saw that she was taller than they had thought, as tall as Arne. She turned her large, dark eyes upon him with an unfathomable expression.

"It was you," she said.

Eight

Arne looked up at her, and then he laughed but there was fear in his laughter. *Either,* he thought, *she has gone mad, or someone has falsely accused me.*

Osan said, "You should not laugh, Arne. Do you not know me well enough by now, even in this short time, to know that I mean exactly what I say?"

He was struck by the change in her eyes: was it pity?

"But I never—I couldn't—" he stammered.

"Yet it was you," she said, firmly. "You have the power of the *tendo*. The same power I have myself."

He grew cold. He found it hard even to draw enough breath into his lungs.

"In the moment when the *crom* struck at you, what did you feel?" said Osan. "You told me that you felt pity for it, that you felt its terror, that you felt almost as if it were human. Your soul is very strong. Now tell me, did you never find in hunting that the feeling for an animal spoiled your shot?"

Arne nodded weakly.

"And so, when you were fighting the *crom* there must

have come a strong thought into your mind, a thought you did not even know you had, a wish that it might have something better than a wooden club with which to oppose your ax. That wish was given reality, and you turned its club into iron by the power of your *tendo*.

"Do you remember when you first saw me, you thanked me? What were you thanking me for?"

"For—for opening the side of the mountain to let us out."

"Just so. But I did nothing. I did not even know where you were until Dag sensed you and ran off to meet you. You did it yourself. Your own wish changed the stone into —who knows what? Grass, a cloud of smoke, thin air."

Arne was conscious that Frey had drawn away from him, and he looked reproachfully at her. "I didn't ask for this," he said.

"Oh, Arne. I'm sorry." She at once moved closer and clasped his hand.

"Don't touch me," he said, bitterly. "I might change your shape without meaning to."

Osan chuckled. "Now you are talking like a fool, without thinking. Think of it as a talent, like the talent of a painter or a carver. You have it, but you don't know what to do with it. It comes unexpectedly now, and only rarely, at a moment of crisis. You must learn how to use it, how to control it."

"Yes, I suppose so." Arne gripped Frey's hand tightly, and put into words what most disturbed him. "Now I will have to live alone on some mountain, as you do, Osan . . . will I?"

She touched his head with a wrinkled hand. "No, my dear, not quite yet. Remember, I told you I once lived with others. The day may come when you will need a solitude like this, but not yet awhile. However, for now, you must stay here with me. I will teach you how to use the *tendo*—and how not to use it."

"And Frey—?"

"Do you expect me to drive her away, down the mountainside?"

Arne took a breath of relief and was able to smile once more. Frey put an arm around his neck and said defiantly, "I wouldn't have let you drive me away in any case."

There began a strange and difficult time of training for Arne, and boredom for Frey. They found that the door in the back wall of the house opened into several chambers within the mountain, one of which had been a room of the ancient people in which Osan had moved away earth and the fallen building stones by her power, to reveal a wall on which a picture had been inlaid with flat colored pebbles in the same way the Horned Man of Strand was made. But this picture showed towering buildings with many windows, and a curious bird with stiff, flat wings in the sky above them. In this room Arne sat with Osan for long hours of every day, learning how to focus his mind, how to make images and concentrate his power to bring them into shape, and a great many complex secrets of the nature of matter and of that mysterious, rhythmical construction which lay beneath all shapes. While he did this, Frey rambled on the mountainside or sat looking at the view when the weather was fine, or dozed indoors when it rained. They ate simply and slept rolled in blankets on the floor of the hut. But for part of every day they listened to Osan's stories of her long life, and learned many things about their world.

They learned that the full power of the *tendo* appeared rarely, and that it seemed to come into readiness for use in a person at about the same time as that person's soul was ready to be awakened. The soul, Osan told them, lay in a central part of the brain in an organ somewhat the size and shape of an eye. More often, people were born who had a little of the *tendo,* not enough to use it to change shapes but enough to heal small wounds, and above all to stir the soul to wakefulness. Such a person was Ness, the youngest member of the council of Strand.

"There are a great many more of such people than there are of those with the complete *tendo,*" said Osan. "Enough of them so that there is hardly a village or town without one or two who can awaken the souls of Unfinished People. But there are never more than a few in each generation with the whole power."

When the power showed itself, or when it was suspected, the councillors of the village or town sent that person with a token to an adept to be trained, as the council of Strand had sent Arne, when the iron club awoke their suspicions. Always the *tendo* was found in a person with a strong soul, a keen ability to picture in his or her mind the life that was in others, and thus it was never used for evil purposes. But the burden of the power was great and grew greater with age, and there had been some who had destroyed themselves rather than go on using it.

There were, Osan told them, only a double handful of people with the *tendo* in the world as they knew it, and a little more than half of them lived in villages or towns. Yet they were able to keep in touch with one another by the use of such companions as Dag.

"Once there were many Dags," Osan explained. "They lived among the ancient people and were fed and petted by them. When that world fell to pieces, just as there were too many people there were also too many Dags, and most of them, unable to fend for themselves, or with too much competition among their own kind, died as their masters had died, and so the Balance was restored.

"Now there are not many of them left. Dag hunts for himself, and goes off for days at a time to be with a pack that lives in the lowlands a little way to the southwest, but I can call him if I have great need of him because his mind and mine are in tune. He has his own name which is known only to other Dags and to me. The Dags seem always to have had a sense of what their masters were thinking, but the *crom* in those days could not speak clearly to them, for masters and slaves do not speak the same language. We who have souls can do so, however, and there is a Dag with each of those of us who has the *tendo*. Over a short distance, I can speak through Dag directly to another mind as I once did to yours. But over great distances my thought will go through my Dag to the Dag of each of the others, and so to their minds, and in this way we can take council when we have to."

Arne had been with Osan now long enough so that the high summer was fading and there were frosts crisping the grass in the morning and making The Pale Woman even paler. He had so far mastered the use of his power as to be able to turn his ax to stone, and then to wood, and had demolished its edge and rebuilt it again, rapidly or slowly at will. He had learned how to wake a soul or still it, how to change the rhythm of matter and turn a snail shell into a living snail or how to open a wound in flesh and heal it up again. And he had spent much time pondering over all that Osan had told him, and all his own experiences. It was as if the use of a power such as was his had changed him, too, not his shape but the shape of his thinking; he was a different Arne from the youth who had set out on this journey.

One morning, Osan said to him, "You have been an apt pupil, Arne. I am well satisfied."

He tried not to look pleased, with so little success that Frey began to laugh, and said, "Look at him, Osan. Surely, people with the *tendo* should be more modest?"

"Don't tease him, Frey," Osan smiled. "Now," she went on, "you are almost ready to leave me. First, you must have a Dag of your own, and we will ask Dag if it is possible that one from his pack might like to join you. Then, I must tell the council about you so that it will be known that there is another of us. And lastly, you must think for a moment where you will go."

"Where I will go? Do you mean I am not to return to Strand?"

Osan shook her head. "You have not considered the

meaning of your power. What will you do with it, now that you have it? Will you go back to your village and live there quietly as a hunter, using the *tendo* to make your arrows?"

"I thought—" Arne began, and stopped, for in fact that was one aspect of things about which he had scarcely thought.

"You are the servant of all Human Beings," Osan said. "You may return to visit Strand if you like, but you must live where you can be found easily by those who need you. You are the newest and youngest of us, and you must serve your apprenticeship as we all did."

Arne felt the weight on his heart. "Must I part from Frey?"

"Not unless she wishes it."

"I don't wish it," said Frey. "I will go with him wherever he goes. He may have the *tendo,* but he still hasn't much sense."

Lightly as she spoke, her voice was full of love and he touched her cheek.

"But where are we to go?" he said, painfully.

"We will speak to the council," said Osan. "Until two years ago, I myself lived in Havens. Ships come and go there, and it can be reached even in winter. There, too, are written records. Can you read?"

"Only trail marks and tallies."

"You must learn. There is a man in Havens, Weikar, who can teach you that and other arts."

He bowed his head. He began to understand, for the first time truly, what she had meant when she had spoken once before of the burden of this power and how some people had killed themselves rather than go on using it. He had, vaguely, thought of himself as settled with Frey in Strand and applying his power to the welfare of his own village, but he saw how childish that had been. To lose the home he loved was not the worst of it. He had thought of his power as giving him new freedom, but it was clear he never would be free again.

"We would have friends in Havens," Frey said, softly.

"Yes," said Arne. He raised his eyes to Osan's. "But I will go where I am sent."

"Good," said the old woman, and her smile was enough to lift his spirits.

She called Dag to her, and taking one of his paws in her hand spoke silently to him. He looked at Arne out of his round, hazel eyes, and Arne felt a message form in his mind, not in words, but in a sense of cheerful assurance. Then Dag gave a bark and bounded away.

"He will try to find you a companion," said Osan.

"I know," Arne said. "I understood him."

"You will discover when you live with a Dag that you will understand each other even better. It will tell you its name, which you must never speak aloud. And remember, your Dag stays with you of its own free will. It will come and go as it likes—and not as you always like. It will eat your food when it can find nothing to hunt, but it will not be your servant. What it does, it will do for friendship toward you and all our race."

"I'll remember," said Arne. A thought struck him. "And

yet the Dags once gave their friendship to the *crom*, didn't they?"

"Why—yes, they did," said Osan, sounding a little surprised.

"Then the *crom* cannot have been utterly wicked," Arne said, half to himself.

They were by then sitting on the bench in front of the hut, for the air was mild although the sky was full of clouds. Below, the color of the forest had begun to change, and among the greens could be seen stains of yellow and crimson, marking patches of birch or maple which had begun to feel the frosts. Somewhere among the trees roamed the band of *crom* which had captured him, and he wondered how they managed when winter came for he could not remember seeing any fire among them.

He said, suddenly, "Do you remember my telling you about Sone?"

Osan nodded.

"Once, when we were talking of the ancient people, you said they mistook the images of things for the things themselves. It seems to me that all of us may do that, sometimes. I have been thinking about Sone, and I think we didn't understand him."

"What was there to misunderstand?" Frey asked. "He had been twisted by being captured by the *crom* when he was young."

"I thought so, too," said Arne. "But I'm no longer sure of it. I have turned it over in my mind, and tried to look at the other side of it. I wonder if he was not twisted when his friends were killed."

"You mean his mother?"

"We don't know that his mother was killed, Frey. He never told us."

"Then what friends do you mean?"

"The *crom*."

Frey looked at him in blank astonishment.

Arne said, "He lived among the *crom* for many years. Don't you remember him telling us that he wandered with them wherever they went, ate what they ate, lived as they lived? He must have played with the young ones—yes, I've seen them playing! He grew up among them. They didn't harm him; they raised him as one of themselves. Then, suddenly, Human Beings found them and killed them all, every one, all those—people—"

"People?"

"Yes, people, with whom he'd lived so long. Why should we think it was the *crom* who twisted him? It may have been we who did it, the Human Beings who killed them."

Arne's face was strained, and both Osan and Frey stared at him, unable to find an argument. He went on, "I've thought of this ever since the night I escaped from them. If Sone had hated the *crom* so, for what they had done to him, he would have gone out hunting them as soon as he received his soul and his ax. But it was Human Beings he killed. Just as he would have killed me."

He had been sitting with his hands locked together, and now he jumped up restlessly and stood looking down into the valley.

"Perhaps we have been wrong," he said. "What if we have been wrong all these years?"

Frey opened her mouth, but Osan silenced her with a gesture. Arne clasped his hands behind his back and stood hunched and motionless for a long time. He turned around, at last, and said, "I have been thinking, too, about the one who cut the cords on my wrists. She knew gratitude, Osan. She knew that we had spared her life, and she wanted me to know she hadn't betrayed me. Therefore, she set me free—and what's more, she gave me back my ax although she knew I might kill her with it. She trusted me. What does that make her? It makes her human, doesn't it? Tell me, Osan!"

"I cannot," Osan said. "The *crom* are not human."

He knelt beside her, resting his hands on her knees as if he were a child. The souls of both Osan and Frey told them clearly what torment he was in, and yet they could not bring themselves to shake off what they had believed all their lives.

"Don't you see," said Arne, "that in her mind that young *crom*—that *girl*—" it was hard for him to say it, but he got the word out, strange as it sounded "—felt what I felt, just as if she had a soul? She saw the picture in her imagination of my suffering. And the white-haired leader of the band—he told me he would eat me, and then he laughed."

"Are you so sure it was laughter?"

"Yes, I'm certain. He laughed, because in the end he didn't eat me after all but he saw in his mind how frightened that made me and he enjoyed the fright. It was—it was like when I was a child, and Gito and I played at frightening each other, jumping out suddenly with a shriek, telling stories to each other of how if we wandered into a certain part of the woods the *crom* would catch us."

"But it—that *crom* you spoke of—it was no child."

"True. He behaved like a child."

"Do children kill each other? The *crom* do, I know they do," said Osan. "I have seen it. I have seen the bodies of their dead, a young one killed by a blow from a stone—"

"Yes," Arne broke in. "It is because they are Unfinished."

Osan sighed. "It cannot be so, Arne. We know from the long records we have kept, we who have the *tendo,* that the ancient people were the ancestors of the *crom.* When the first Human Beings appeared, people with souls, they knew that they would have to destroy the *crom* to prevent their ever conquering the earth again. Would you want them to breed in their thousands, to build up their cities, to fight their wars, to kill us and each other, the animals, the plants, the soil itself, as they did long ago?"

"No," said Arne, in a low voice. He sat still, thinking, and added, "But there is another way to tell it. Suppose we are all *crom?*"

He looked from Osan to Frey, and continued, "Wait. Let me say this. Once you told us that people with the *tendo* were brought into being by the spirit of Harmony. They were needed, to bring things into balance. They awoke the soul in others, you said. But in how many could they awaken it? There were not many of them, and they could only awaken the soul in a few others, as many as they could reach. Then, from generation to generation there would be more and more people with souls—but there would be thousands in whom the soul still lay asleep. They would be people always Unfinished. They would have, buried in their brains, the organ where the soul lies but it would never be stirred to life. They would see in their minds a dim picture of how others felt, but never clearly enough to stop them from acting in pure selfishness, for themselves alone. Never enough to keep them from murder. Is that possible?"

He gazed deeply at her, and Osan answered, reluctantly, "It is possible."

"If those Unfinished people were driven into the forests and hunted by those whose souls were awakened, they would become worse than ever. They would hate us, and long for revenge. They attacked the village of Chestnuts not because they wanted to steal the crops but because they wanted to destroy them. Why not? We are their enemies. Their brothers, and their enemies."

He touched the thong he wore around his neck, from which hung the coup he had taken in the raid on Chestnuts, the disk of pearly shell. "Some of us," he said, "wear black cone shells to show that we have killed *crom*. But that killing is itself a dangerous pleasure. We could have acted long ago all together to exterminate them, but we didn't. We kill them only when we find them. It is almost as if—as if we wanted some of them to remain, so that we could keep the joy of killing. We are seeing the image but not the truth beneath, that they are ourselves as we might be without souls."

Osan shivered. The clouds had darkened and the air was growing chilly and smelled of rain.

"I am cold," she said. "Let us go inside. I must think of what you have said."

"I—" Arne began.

She interrupted him. "Don't speak any more of it now."

She looked so stern and forbidding that he said no more. Even Frey didn't venture to speak, and they passed an uncomfortable hour seated before the fireplace in which Osan, with no more than a casual glance, made a handful of stones become blazing logs. Rain began to patter on the roof and Arne closed the shutters. They could hear it streaming in the wooden gutter and splashing on the ground, and all he could think of was the sound of weeping.

At length, Osan stirred, and in her usual kindly, humorous tone, said, "Forgive me, both of you, if I have frightened you. You needn't cringe away any longer. It is growing late, go and fetch some dinner from the storeroom."

They hastened to do as she said, bringing a jug of milk, a green-veined cheese, a bowl of raisins and walnuts, and a loaf of coarse brown bread to the table. They sat down on their stools and began to eat.

Osan said, "You have given me a great deal to think about, Arne. More than I have had in my head for many years. It seems to me that what you say may be true."

He felt no triumph, only great despondency, for if it were true then there lay on all Human Beings a dark weight of hundreds of years of death, as much guilt surely as that which could be laid to the ancestors of the *crom* for all their murders. And then he told himself that if he was right the ancestors of the *crom* were those of humanity, as well, and the guilt was shared by all alike.

"I have considered everything," Osan went on, "and I think we must speak to the council. We cannot do that until Dag returns, so let us finish our meal peacefully and forget everything until then."

"I can't forget any of it," Arne said.

Frey pressed her cheek to his. "Nor I," she murmured. "If it can be the truth, then we are no better than the *crom* —no, we are worse. I have a medicine with me that will make us both sleep."

"No," said Osan. "I can do better than that."

Bending forward, she took Arne's face between her hands. She touched her forehead to his and sat back. "There," she said.

Arne looked at her, knitting his brows. All memory of their talk about the *crom* had gone out of his mind. He knew that they had been discussing something—something as dreadful as it was important, which had disturbed him, but he couldn't remember what it was.

"Why did you say, 'There'?" he said. "What were we talking about?"

"It was nothing," Osan answered.

"What have you done?" asked Frey.

"This," she replied, and touched her forehead to Frey's. Frey blinked, looked as if she were about to speak, and smiled instead in bewilderment.

"Now, if you like," said Osan, briskly, "we will clear away the dishes and cups and Frey shall sing us one of Bakko's romantic dance-poems which she likes so much, or one of Harad's tales of the Sea Lord which I like so much, perhaps the Tale of the Seven Barrels."

"Whichever you like," said Frey, "or both."

That night's sleep was deep and dreamless for the pair, and whatever Osan had done to their memory persisted until late the following morning. The old woman came to Arne, where he was sitting in one of the chambers inside the mountain practicing the use of the *tendo,* changing a flat stone into a round one, then into a lump of gold, and then into a glowing coal. She touched his forehead with hers, and all that he had forgotten came rushing back to him. At a wave of his hand, the coal became stone.

"Frey?" he said.

"I have restored her memory, as well. Dag has returned. Come outside."

Dag was sitting on the grass before the hut, his tongue lolling out over his teeth and dripping from his running. Beside him sat panting another Dag, a bitch, as big as he but slenderer, with an air of suppleness and grace, but with something fierce about her instead of Dag's jauntiness. As soon as he saw her, Arne liked her and felt a little afraid of her. It was, in fact, not unlike what he felt about Osan.

Her strange, savage mind touched his, knowing no words but first questioning, then with contentment. He saw, in his imagination, a fleeting image, blurred but gradually coming into focus, quite flat, in shades of gray, of a tall, two-legged creature and another on four legs running side by side. He recognized himself and the female Dag. A faint, acrid scent came to his nostrils and translated itself in his mind into a kind of name: Rrek. He almost said it aloud and remembered that he must not do so. The bitch, however, gave a short bark of satisfaction and with a start he realized that she had said—or tried to say— *Arne.*

"Very good," said Osan. "You will get along well together. Now, if the Dags are willing, we will go to the inner chamber and call our council. Not you, Frey," she added. "You had better remain here, outside."

Frey had been watching Arne with the female Dag beside him. She snapped, "Oh, yes, of course. I must always be outside, mustn't I?"

Arne glanced at her in surprise for her tone was more than petulant; there was real anger in it. In the same instant, his soul and hers touched and he understood everything. She had been more than patient, and she had endured boredom and jealousy, waiting for him to complete his training, knowing that he had a power she could never have, and uttering no word of complaint.

He strode to her side, taking her by the shoulders. She tried to evade him, but he held her fast, looking deeply into her eyes.

"Well?" she said, sullenly.

"I've been taught to change many things but I can't change this. Neither what I have, nor what there is between us, Frey. Must I be like Osan and—and dance alone?"

She gripped his wrists, and her lips tightened. "No, you'll never be alone if I can help it. But why must *I* be alone?"

"It's what his power demands," Osan put in, in a somber voice. "He no longer belongs to himself, Frey, nor to you."

"You have always been quicker than I," Arne said, gently. "Be quicker now, to understand."

She gave a heavy sigh. "I do understand. But understanding is a poor food when you're hungry."

She drew him to her and kissed him. Then she pulled away and sat down on the bench with her face averted.

Osan led the way to the room with the colored stone picture on the wall. She pointed to a block of stone; it became a chair with a high back. She nodded to Arne who, not without some nervousness under the eyes of both Dags, made a similar seat for himself. Osan closed her eyes, Dag lay down at her feet, and for a long time both seemed almost to be asleep.

Abruptly, her eyelids snapped open and she looked at Arne. A voice, which although he could not hear it he knew to be both deep and resonant, spoke in his mind: *I am Thorar.*

Another said, *Gerya.*

Another and another. He lost count, but he knew from what Osan had told him that there were twenty-two. He knew also that he was hearing their thoughts sent through their own Dags to Rrek, who now sat beside him with her muzzle on his thigh. A vague, confusing knowledge of all those Dags lay like an undertone to the other voices, making as it were a faint growling note.

He recognized Osan's voice as the others faded. She began to tell the story of his own adventures from the time of the raid and the fight with the *crom* to the moment when he had come to her. She used images as well as words, and often whole episodes, as if they were memories from Arne's own brain, streamed through his imagination like dreams. She went on, then, and described all that had happened since, and repeated the conversation in which Arne had spoken of the possibility that the *crom* were Unfinished Human Beings who might possess the organ of the soul but had never had it awakened. She omitted nothing, yet so swift was thought that only a short time seemed to elapse before she was done.

For a moment there was a confusion of words in Arne's head, and a babble of emotion which swept through him so that he felt amazement, horror, indignation, even a tinge of rage, all at once. It ended, and his mind was empty.

After a pause, a voice which, even in silence, was piercingly sweet, said, *I cannot believe what you tell me and yet I must believe that it is possible. I can find no answer but one. The thing must be tried.*

Arne looked at Rrek, and his own reply sped out before the words for it could properly form in his brain. *I know,* he thought. *I have known it from the beginning. I will go.*

Nine

Frey had set up a peeled stick as a target and was shooting at it in competition with herself, first holding the bow in her left hand and then in her right. When Arne came out of the hut, she looked once at his face and said, "What's wrong?"

He said, haltingly, "I'm—I must go down into the valley, to find the *crom.*"

"It has something to do with this idea of yours—"

"Yes." He gulped in a breath and went on, "I'm going alone, Frey."

"You're not."

"I must. I haven't any choice."

Her cheeks began to burn. "You can't go alone. They'll kill you. You're leaving me outside again."

"No. Not that. Never that. Please listen to me, Frey." He took her hand, and the anguish in his tone dissolved her own pain. "You taught me to think ahead and make plans, just as you did long ago when we went on the raid to Chestnuts. I've thought about this. If two of us go they'll think we're hunting them, and I'll have no chance whatever. They will either ambush us or run away. I must get close to them and somehow make them listen to me. If we both go there will be too much danger of a fight, a wrong move."

Her eyes suddenly blurred and the tears burst out. "Why must you do it, Arne? What do you care about the *crom?* What difference does it make if they live or die?"

"You don't mean that."

"No," she said, sadly. "I'm afraid for your sake."

"You forget," Osan said, "that he has a stronger weapon now than any ax."

"I have the best of weapons," Arne said. "I no longer hate them."

He laid his ax on the bench. "I'll come back for this," he said.

Frey embraced him, kissing him fiercely. "You'd better," she said. "If you don't, I'll—"

"—do as Osan tells you," Arne finished for her. "Let me go, now."

Reluctantly he turned away from her. Osan kissed him farewell, solemnly. He set off at a long stride around the shoulder of the mountain, not looking back.

He made his way downward at an angle to the slope, passing the gaping crack through which he and Frey had come, weeks before, and casting no more than a casual glance at it. He no longer felt any curiosity about what was inside; he knew it now for a place of the dead. The tall grass was drying and the steep incline was slippery. He had to go carefully, zigzagging back and forth as he descended until he came to a saddle where the hills on the west met the flank of The Pale Woman. Here he turned inward toward the valley. The way down was easier, with angular boulders jutting out now and then on which he could rest. He recognized, from their texture, that they were shaped stones from the ancient buildings. He was sitting on one, catching his breath, when he became aware that he was no longer alone. Rrek was sitting on the ground a little way behind him.

He thought at her: *Go back.*

She yawned, her yawn ending in a squeak. He felt her flat refusal.

You can do nothing, he said.

She grinned, showing deadly white teeth. He understood.

No one is to be bitten, he said, firmly.

Her reply formed itself in his head, not in speech but in the instant knowledge that if he wished to send a message to Osan, Rrek would be there for him to do so.

"Ah, well," he said, aloud, "it makes it less lonely. Come on, then."

They descended to the valley floor. They walked among bushes which had lost most of their leaves and on which the clusters of waxy, white berries were now a brilliant crimson. Arne stared from side to side, searching for some trace of the *crom* and, as he did so, resolutely forcing down his anxiety. They could be watching him from some hidden spot and before he could make a move to defend himself, a stone or a club could come flying and put an end to him. The further he went, however, the more he began to worry in the other direction, that the band he was looking for might have moved on, might be a hundred miles away by now.

He felt Rrek's cold nose nudge his thigh. He looked down at her, gathering her thought: she was saying that if he wanted to find the *crom* he must follow her. And even before he could wonder why, her reply came. Good as his sense of smell was, hers was far better. She could scent the *crom* in the distance. She trotted ahead, and he followed at an easy hunter's lope. They left the valley and entered the fringe of the forest. Bright leaves lay here and there among the dry ferns, rustling occasionally under Arne's light sandals.

He could smell the *crom* himself, now, and a few moments later he saw them. He slowed his steps and Rrek dropped back to walk demurely behind him. The band was gathered around something on the ground, and when he got closer he saw that they had brought down a deer. The white-haired one was standing at its head, while two of the other males expertly skinned it. The rest watched patiently. Arne was downwind of them and they were not instantly aware of him.

He moved slightly to the right. The leader glimpsed the motion from the corner of his eye and whirled, snarling. The rest, alarmed, turned as quickly, clubs ready.

Arne held up both his hands, fingers spread wide to show that he held no weapon. He could see the puzzlement in the leader's eyes. One of the males, however, crouching and showing his teeth, hurled a club.

Arne saw it leave the *crom*'s hand. In that split second, he focused his power as he had been taught. In midair the club flew apart in a burst of white. A cloud of small, curling feathers floated to the grass.

The *crom* shrank back, pressing together, too frightened to utter more than a few whimpering noises. Even the leader drew away, gripping his club more tightly. They were poised between fascination at what he might do next and panic. Arne knew that he must hold them or they would run off in terror. Yet he dared not make any sudden move.

He thought of the thong around his neck, with the coup hanging from it. Slowly, carefully, he took the pearly disk in his hand. Thong and disk vanished; he felt the stirring in his palm as their shape changed, and when he opened his hand a large butterfly clung there, unfurling its wings, deep purple and yellow, shimmering in the sunlight. A long *ooh!* came from many of the *crom,* and one of the little ones laughed, a recognizable human laugh.

"I will not harm you," Arne said, in his gentlest voice. "There is no danger."

Looking from face to face, he saw more curiosity than fear. Some of them, at least, understood him. On the edge of the group, he saw a face he knew, that of the young female who had cut his bonds. So she was still alive, he thought with relief; they had not connected her with his escape. The butterfly had climbed to one of his fingers. Very slowly, he walked forward holding it out.

The band moved cautiously away as he advanced, all but the girl. She smiled timidly at him. Her arm, he saw, was nearly healed but still showed four raking scars. He shook his hand lightly, and the butterfly flew off. A couple of the little ones, their fright completely gone, ran after it with joyous yells. Arne went up to the girl, returning her smile. She did not move. He ran his fingers down her arm. The scars melted away.

The rest of the band gathered closer, jostling each other to stare, some of the women cheeping to each other in undertones. The big, white-haired leader shoved his way through among them. He glared at Arne from under his bristling brows but he no longer threatened. Instead, he pointed at Arne with a gnarled finger on which the nail was like a talon.

"Why?" he growled.

Arne said, "I can't explain. We have no words between us—or too many words. How can I show you?"

The way to do it was to try to awaken his soul—if he had one. From all that he had seen so far, Arne felt that there was hope. Hairy and savage the *crom* might be but their behavior was, he told himself, more human than otherwise. However, it was that of a humanity in which the soul slept, in which each one lived in an interior lone-liness, unable to feel as others felt except in the weakest, faintest way. And yet—and yet, Arne thought, he might still be wrong. The centuries might have withered up that gland in the brain in which the soul lay, so that it could no longer be stimulated. Or the surface might be human but below it another kind of being might lurk, one in which there never could be a soul.

If he was to try at all, he must try with the leader. But among Human Beings, so far as he knew, the soul was always awakened at a certain age, fifteen or sixteen at the latest. Did he dare try with someone as old as this?

He knew, without turning to look, that Rrek was somewhere nearby. *Osan,* he thought. He felt a moment's confusion—almost, he would have said, a *barking* in his mind—and then, soundlessly, Osan's voice saying, *I am here.*

Swiftly the thoughts ran between them:

Can the soul be awakened in an older person?

How old? Not as old as I am.

I don't know. Perhaps three times my age.

There is a time which is best. But if the seat of the soul is there, and unharmed—if the blood still runs freely in the veins—

I don't know . . .

He gazed at the *crom,* who stood as before. The whole exchange with Osan had lasted no more than a second or two. He had an answer but it did him little good. He would have to risk it.

He went up close to the white-haired one, so close that the outstretched finger touched his breast. The *crom* frowned, opening his palm as if to ward Arne off, but he neither gave ground nor seemed angry. He was waiting.

Arne said, "Will you trust me?"

"Eh?" grunted the *crom.* "Trust?"

"I will not hurt you."

"Not hurt?"

Hesitantly, Arne reached out his hand. The white-haired one flinched, and then stood still again, waiting to see what would happen. Arne touched the mat of coarse, white hair. His eyes held those of the *crom* as he probed with his fingers to find that spot on the top of the skull which Osan had shown him. His power, so much greater than that of Ness who had brought his own soul to life in the initiation ceremony, needed no such effort as hers and he knew that there would be none of the pain he himself had felt. But what would be felt? Nothing at all?

He closed his eyes for a moment, seeking the Balance within himself, and then thought, *Wake!*

The *crom* started back, away from his hand, with a shout. Arne's eyes flew open. He felt a thrill of horror for it had seemed to him that there was distress in that cry and that he had failed.

He knew in the next instant that he had not failed, for he was looking into the eyes of a Human Being.

Nothing else had changed. The hulking body, the hairiness, the long arms, the rank odor all remained as before. But it was no longer a *crom* who stood before him, but a man. He felt what Arne felt, and he was linked by that understanding to the rest of humanity. He looked at the club he still held, and then at Arne. The club fell to the ground. He held out both his hands and Arne took them, and they smiled at each other.

The white-haired man gazed about him. The rest of the band had drawn away at the shout but had not fled. "Them?" he said to Arne.

"Yes," said Arne. "All but the children. They must wait a while. And there is so much to show you."

He hardly knew how to begin. He would have to take council with Osan at once so that she could spread word of what had happened, among all those with the *tendo*.

When Arne had awakened the souls of the others in the band, he would have to bring them to a village where they could be shown the ways of humanity. And that was only the beginning, for the *crom* would have to be searched out everywhere, protected from death, and changed into Human Beings.

They would have to have axes, too. But the ax would never again be anything but an emblem of brotherhood.

He gripped the hard, grimy hands with their claw-like nails.

"Welcome!" he said, his voice catching on the word. "Welcome!"

Jay Williams has been a professional author for over thirty years, with more than sixty-five books to his credit. They range through fiction and non-fiction for children and adults. Among them are the popular *Danny Dunn* books, two of which have won the PNLA Young Readers' Award; the series is published in England and Japan as well as the United States. Mr. Williams has written picture-story books, historical novels and fantasy for young readers. His most recent fantasies are *The Hawkstone* and *The Hero from Otherwhere*. His adult books include *Tomorrow's Fire, The Forger, Uniad* and *Stage Left,* while under the name of Michael Delving he is known for his crime novels.

Jay Williams divides his time between a village in Gloucestershire, England, and a village in Connecticut. He is married and has two children, one a musician, the other a silversmith.